SNOWBALL

By the Same Author

A CHOICE OF ENEMIES

TED ALLBEURY

SNOWBALL

J. B. LIPPINCOTT COMPANY
PHILADELPHIA / NEW YORK

U.S. Library of Congress Cataloging in Publication Data

Allbeury, Ted.
    Snowball.

    I. Title.
PZ4.A415Sn3 [PR6051.L52]   823'.9'14   73–19974
ISBN–0–397–01020–6

To my much-loved children,
David, Kerry, Lisa, and Sally

You should understand, therefore, that there are two ways of fighting: by law or by force. The first way is natural to men, and the second to beasts. But as the first way often proves inadequate one must needs have recourse to the second. So a prince must understand how to make a nice use of the beast and the man.

—MACHIAVELLI

SNOWBALL

1

MICHELE MARLOWE, or Ethel Bates as her mom knew her, was the proud owner of a 38-inch bust. She was also a bit tired. She was the last performer on the late-late show at the Lotus Strip Club, the fourth from the corner of London's Soho Lane and Wardour Street. Unlike her sisters in show biz, the last act wasn't the top of the bill because the late-late show generally brought in a handful of gentlemen who were more interested in the friendly haze than the art of the stripper. Nevertheless, off-duty waiters, drug pushers, and the flotsam of Soho knew a good strip when they saw one, but Ethel tended to rest on the laurels of her effulgent charms. She was aware too that the little bastard on the lights didn't like her and there was a spotlight on a certain place that showed that Ethel had not had a steady hand with the razor—for Ethel, good mornings had not begun with Gillette—and all round, Ethel was not pleased.

It was nearly 2 A.M. when she got back to her place at D'Arbley Street, and as soon as she switched on the light she saw the money on the mantelpiece: four pound notes and nine 10p coins. The tenth coin was in her bag, a terrible reminder of London's wicked ways. Only that afternoon one of her gentleman friends—anyone who stayed for an hour was a friend—had been short of notes but heavy on loose change. But she'd accepted the coins with charm—"It's all bread, duckie"—and when he'd left she'd gone to stick one of the coins in the electricity meter, and it had split in two. It was rather well done, all hollowed out inside and a little piece of celluloid stuck inside like a motto in a fortune cooky. But Ethel preferred paper hats to mottoes, and she didn't like jokes that ruined good money.

Early on Sunday evening Detective Constable Lovejoy called on Ethel. Lovejoy was a member of the Metropolitan Police Vice Squad, but as a typical *New Statesman* reader he had a warm spot in his heart for "those rejects of a materialist society who gave up the unequal struggle"; he had quite a warm spot too for 38-inch busts. Some girls said if you once opened your legs for a copper there's no end to it, but Ethel reckoned that her mom was right and a friend in need was a friend indeed. And there was no doubt that DC Lovejoy was in need—generally on Sunday afternoons.

Again, as Ethel often said, "When they've done it, all they want's a cuppa tea." It was while they were having the cup of tea that Ethel showed Lovejoy the phony 10p coin. He recognized roughly what its contents were in two seconds and took five seconds more to concoct a cover story for when he took his find back to Albany Street. He gave Ethel 50p in exchange.

In the stop-press column of the final edition of Monday's *Evening Standard* there was a four-line piece which said that the assistant cook from the Polish passenger ship MV *Batory* had applied for political asylum in Britain as he "was disgusted with the policies of the Soviet Union." The Home Secretary was considering the case. And although it was barely legible in most copies of the *Evening Standard*, they did print it, appropriately enough, in red.

For the fourth time in two days a man examined the metal tag that said *Dianthus barbatus* on a flowerbed in

Kensington Gardens and for the fourth time said, *"Cholera przekleta,"* which is something not very nice in Polish.

The Polish Embassy in Weymouth Street was, as they say in the Royal Navy, lit overall. The departing French Ambassador was due at eight, and there was much to be done. The Polish Ambassador himself was never at his best on these occasions and always had half an hour of quiet in his own office to prepare a few *bons mots* in whatever language would be appropriate for the evening. After two years as Polish Representative at the United Nations, that gentle backwater had taught him that a good Latin tag was acceptable, in dire need, to all except the Americans. For the first ten minutes this evening he'd been weighing the merits of *"beatus ille qui procul negotiis . . . paterna rure bobus exercet suis,"* but there was a touch of Khrushchev about it, so for safety's sake he settled on *"auspicium melioris aevi,"* at which he reckoned nobody could take offense.

He'd only just lit his cigar when there was a peremptory knock on the door. With a sigh he said, "Come in."

To his surprise it was his chauffeur, Pawel Krezki, and even more to his surprise Krezki sat himself down without a by-your-leave and proceeded to pound his fist on the table.

"What the hell is being done about the man from the *Batory?*"

Up to this point His Excellency had been under the impression that he was one of the few Iron Curtain country ambassadors who had a chauffeur who actually was a chauffeur. But he'd been an ambassador for seven years and he could read the signs as quickly as the next man. He spoke very quietly.

"Comrade Krezki, I think you would be wise to establish your position with me."

Krezki said, "If you look in your safe, comrade,

you'll remember a red envelope with seals—please open it."

A few minutes later it was open on His Excellency's desk. There was just a sheet of good, stiff, white note-paper which simply announced to all concerned that comrade chauffeur Pawel Krezki was also Major Krezki of Z-11, the Polish version of the Russians' KGB. It didn't go on to request help of any kind because it didn't need to. Majors in Z-11 were not ten a penny in any-body's currency. The letter went back in its envelope and the envelope back in the safe.

"So, Major, what about the defector? A protest has been lodged with the British Home Secretary, and of course we have asked for access. There is nothing more we can do at the moment." He put his hands palm down on his desk as if getting ready to rise, but Krezki was red in the face with anger.

"Borowski, I want that man. I want him here and I want him quick, and that's your responsibility. I don't want to report adversely on your cooperation, so I want that man."

But Ambassador Borowski was not without influence himself—in Moscow as well as Warsaw—and wasn't to be bullied even by intelligence majors. So he stood up, put his arm around Krezki's shoulder, and headed him to the door.

"Comrade Major, an ambassador has many responsibilities. We must not look too eager or the British will be suspicious."

He was tempted to ask for his car to be brought around, but maybe that would be too provocative. Levit-ski in Paris had been clobbered for less.

When Lovejoy brought his little peace offering to Detective Inspector Lowrie, he had a slightly unpleasant ten minutes.

"And how come you were at this tom's place on a Sunday afternoon, Lovejoy?"

"Well, sir, the girl has assisted me with inquiries on a number of occasions."

"You've entered these facts in the Incidents Book on the appropriate dates, have you?"

"Yes, sir."

"Right. Let's see it."

A few minutes later the Inspector looked up from the ledger.

"I'll tell you what, Lovejoy. There's too many bloody Sundays for my liking." He wagged one of Her Majesty's pencils at the embarrassed Lovejoy. "I'm warning you, lad, you just bloody well lay off or you'll find yourself in the bloody 'News of the World' one of these fine Sunday mornings, and I don't mean a commendation from the Chief Constable either. It'll be one of those investigations by 'our special reporter' that starts off about 'lovely blonde starlet' and ends up with 'at this point our investigator made an excuse and left the premises.' When you want it, have it on some other patch, not mine." Then, perhaps feeling his underling might be regretting reporting his find, he added without looking up, "You'd not go far wrong in Brighton—have a word with Sergeant Watkins there. Now I want a written report on this lot before you go off duty tonight."

A photostat of the report and the coin itself went off to Commander Bryant at Special Branch an hour later.

2

THE THREE FRENCHMEN booked in at half-hourly intervals at the London Hilton but all on the same floor. They were registered as Pierrre Firette, *commerçant,* André Prouvost, *écrivain,* and Paul Loussier, *ingénieur.* They met together later in the tearoom, and after complaining to the waiter about the quality of the mille-feuilles they got down to business. Prouvost confirmed that he was quite sure that *Le Monde* would print, provided they saw photostats of the documents. All three agreed that there would be no contact with the French Embassy. And Firette was to be the contact with the Poles.

"Let me just write down a few details, Miss Bates. It's Miss Ethel Bates, isn't it?"

"Ethel Sandra Bates in full, actually."

"And where were you born?"

"Seventy-two Abinger Gardens, Stepney."

"Age?"

"Twenty." She saw him hesitate with his pen poised, and when he looked up she said, "Well, that's my stage bit, like—legally, so to speak, I'm twenty-five —but," she added, "I don't mind you knowing, of course, Commander." She rather liked the Commander, and she reckoned that Special Branch was a lot dishier than the Vice Squad.

"Now tell me about this man and what happened—just an outline," he added hastily. When she'd said her piece he said, "You've given me a very good physical description. Now, what about personal mannerisms?"

"Well, I'd say he was foreign—you know, a bit bowing and scraping, like. He kissed my hand twice—that was beforehand, of course—and he wasn't very good with the money. He knew the quid notes, but I had to help him with the coins."

"And you're quite sure you'd never seen him before?"

"No, he was new, all right."

"And how did you meet him?"

"Well, I just went to the bottom of the stairs for a breath of fresh air and he kept walking past—about four or five times—and I could see he was interested, and then he came up and propositioned me."

"Did he have an accent? What did he say exactly?"

The big blue eyes were lowered for a moment to her lap, but she looked him in the eye when she said, "He just said, 'How much?'"

Commander Bryant closed his notebook. "You've been very helpful, Miss Bates. I much appreciate it."

She brightened up immediately. "How about a nice cuppa before you go?"

"Never been known to refuse a nice cuppa, Miss Bates."

She stood up, pushing down her skirt so that it almost covered her bottom, swept two enamel mugs from the mantelpiece, and marched across to a half-open door. She left it wide open, and Commander Bryant faced one of those tests of initiative that are not covered at the Police College. As Miss Bates bent over it became obvious that not only was she not wearing any pants but that she had one of the most luscious bottoms that he'd ever had the pleasure of regarding. But the initiative bit came when he realized that she'd just pulled the chain and was delicately cleaning the two mugs in the flushing toilet bowl. He rose hurriedly.

"Miss Bates, on second thoughts I ought not to accept your kind hospitality. This might end up with some publicity, and you never know what the papers could make of an innocent cup of tea."

Thank God for a vigilant press, he thought. Where should we all be without their protection?

The Third Secretary at the Polish Embassy was the only member of the staff who was not a member of the Party, but Ambassador Borowski always found him most useful when dealing with the British. Third Secretary Suslik had been a fighter pilot with a Polish squadron in the RAF. He seemed to understand the British and their devious ways and could get things done that with more formal diplomatic approaches seemed to get bogged down.

When Suslik made an informal request to the Foreign Office to interview the defector from the MV *Batory*, he was invited to meet him in the presence of a senior official, with cups of tea all around.

At the FO they were used to the browbeating and threats against families that served as interviews by Iron Curtain diplomats with their defecting compatriots, so Suslik made a good impression. He had recognized immediately that the man was some sort of operator in one of the Z-11 apparats in Britain, but he kept the conversation relaxed and friendly. When he eventually asked for five minutes on his own with the defector, he was at least listened to.

"What have you got in mind, Mr. Suslik?"

"Well, I'm quite convinced that this man does wish to stay in this country, and bearing that in mind I feel I've done my duty and we should withdraw. His criti-

18

cisms are not entirely unfounded—my country has suffered much and we are still struggling to survive; nevertheless, I'm interested in his real reasons because I'm sure we've only heard part of the story. I think he'd probably relax more on his own with me. I'd like to try. We've got to hear the dissidents if we want to improve things."

The FO had already decided that the defector was probably getting out from under some emotional problem and was of no propaganda use, so Suslik was given his five minutes.

When the door had closed he leaned back in his chair and said, "Well, now that we're on our own, Zygmund, tell me what it's really all about. I think I shall recommend that you are worried about something personal and that you should be allowed to stay. We can make things easy, you know, as well as difficult."

Zygmund Kujawski already half regretted his impulsive move and thought he could now see a chance of keeping a foot in both camps. He lowered his voice almost to a whisper.

"I'd got instructions to place two coins in certain places," he started, and then retailed the episode with the girl and the mix-up with the coins. Suslik memorized the details carefully, and they ended up laughing together at the silly things that could alter one's life. He reassured Kujawski and then had a word with the FO man and told him that it was apparently some silly affair with a girl that had gone wrong.

The tape of the conversation was translated and transcribed into English about two hours later and was with Special Branch just after lunch.

And Ambassador Borowski passed on the bad news about Kujawski to Major Pawel Krezki.

In a third-floor room at the slum end of King's

Road, Pawel Krezki slit open the brown paper wrapper from a copy of *Paris Match* and turned to the first page of editorial. He held the page slantwise to the light and there it was, a shiny full stop. He touched it with a razor blade, easing it up from the glossy paper, and it came away smoothly.

There must be Communist agents who actually use talcum powder, because they all have a tin of the stuff. It's the KGB's standard place to hide a microdot reader.

When the reader was assembled and the microdot centered, Krezki shone the light across the thin film and the text sprang up clear and sharp. It was a letter from his wife, Ilse, the usual stuff—how much she was missing him, how well the boys were doing at school, could he spare another 200 zlotys a month, and had he found her a white dress with a tight bodice and sequins on the flared skirt? The KGB and Z-11 liked to keep families in touch, but this was the second letter he'd had from home in two months and that was more than the usual going rate. He wondered what it all added up to. Could mean they were happy. Could mean they were having doubts. But they'd given him this special assignment— he was almost working for the KGB. They couldn't have heard yet that the courier was with the British, unless that bastard ambassador had signaled back the news. Until he had the microfilm he couldn't make a move. He couldn't even contact the Frenchmen. He dropped the microdot into the stove. It hardly flared, even on the hot coal.

In Fort George Meade in Maryland it was three in the morning, and Hank Peters parked his Pontiac GTO in the staff lot and handed in the keys at the external checkpoint. It was going to be a fine day but hadn't made it yet. One guard was checking his pass and identity card and the other stood by with a light machine gun pointing at Peters' legs. The barbed-wire fence was ten feet high. The same procedure took place at the second guardhouse with a similar fence.

Ex-Naval Lieutenant Peters was a mathematician, not a sailor, and he had now worked eighteen months in subdivision ADVA, one of the five subdivisions of PROD, the most important part of the United States National Security Agency. There was always round-the-clock work at NSA, and Peters had been called in for a rush job and had booked time on the new Whirlwind computer specially developed for NSA as a number cruncher. It was reckoned that Whirlwind could break a code in an hour that would take a first-class mathematician at least three hundred years.

NSA breaks the codes of all foreign governments, friendly or otherwise. And with more than 2,000 radio intercept stations planted around the globe, it monitors radio communications in every country in the world. It was thanks to NSA monitors that Dulles knew two minutes before Khrushchev about the trouble which developed on Gary Powers' U-2 when it was approaching Sverdlovsk; the monitors had taped the voices of the Russian gun crews reporting the plane's maneuvers. Armies and navies have to communicate, and whether it's in code or in clear, NSA listens and tapes. In 4.2 seconds it can give the whereabouts and activities of any service unit in any armed force in the world.

There was half an hour to go before Peters could access his terminal to Whirlwind, and he looked over the columns of five-digit numbers on the ten-by-eight-inch glossy photograph. It gave an impression of one of those one-word randomly added codes, but he was too experienced to let his first thoughts jell. He'd put it through the first three standard routines, and after that he could try some fancy stuff. He checked again on the typed instructions that came with the job. He already knew it was for the British through the CIA, and the instructions made clear that although it was routine because it didn't have classification above Top Secret, it did have 4A's priority. And it was to go by hand to CIA HQ at Langley Field, Virginia, just outside Washington.

Then his red light was blinking and he tapped out the basic data on his terminal and left the computer to run through Programs 1, 2, and 3, which would involve accessing to several thousand million items of stored data 360 separate times.

The line printer was fast by normal computer standards, but even 1,000 characters a second left the printer working after the computer had finished all three programs. The computer took nearly ninety-five seconds and the printer took five minutes. Peters had been half right; it was a two-word random code, but there was something odd about it. He set it up to check the language, and the answer caused him to phone the Whirlwind computer control room. It was going to be a bastard—it was a two-language code. He'd need at least another two hours of computer time. He asked for a partition and got it.

It was, in fact, nearly three hours later when he broke the code. There had actually been two sets of twelve characters, each representing the same word in two languages, *Pilkasniezna* in Polish and *Bouledeneige* in French. In both languages it meant "snowball." He decoded the groups carefully, raised his eyebrows at the final text, and double-sealed the finished material.

There were two messengers to take the package to CIA headquarters, which was normal routine. NSA trusted nobody, and all material that left the building was taken by two individuals who never left each other until the delivery was completed.

The fine day had definitely made it when the package arrived at Langley.

Commander Bryant was almost at the top of Sanderstead Hill when he stopped. He was not an emotional

22

man, but he said out loud, looking up at the stars in the deep blue night sky, "What a stupid, stupid sod!" A lady with a poodle who was about to emerge from her garden gate backed slowly up her garden path.

As soon as he was home Bryant apologized to his long-suffering wife and phoned his office. The duty officer dispatched a car immediately, and an hour later he told the driver to stop in Shaftesbury Avenue and pick him up at the same spot in an hour.

When he got to D'Arbley Street there was a light on in the girl's flat. He rang the bell and looked at his watch—3 A.M. He rang again and there was still no answer, but he thought he could hear voices. With the aid of a plastic credit card the lock came open, and he went up the stairs and listened outside the door. There were voices, but they were too indistinct for him to hear the words. He knocked on the door and then turned the handle. The door opened. There was a soft pink light from the bedside lamp, and the radio was tuned to the all-night program on France-Inter. It seemed there'd been a fatal accident on the Paris–Melun road. There'd been a fatality here as well. The girl was naked and lying on her side, her hands cradling her head on the pillow. Her lips were drawn back from her teeth in a rictus, and as he gently turned her on her back there was a rush of gases from the slit that ran from her sternum to her pelvis.

He sighed and turned to look for what he'd come to check on. The pound notes were still there on the mantelpiece, but there were only eight 10p coins. The front of the electricity meter had been smashed off, and on the floor in front of the meter were four shillings and one old two-shilling piece. The coins on the mantelpiece were no longer in a pile. And they were all genuine. After he'd phoned to Scotland Yard he looked around. There was nothing to interest him. He'd get the Murder Squad preliminary by the time he was awake.

3

THE CABINET MEETING which had been arranged for ten that morning had been canceled and the Prime Minister driven down to a house near Petersfield in Hampshire. The house was set in its own fifty acres of parkland and was the headquarters of Electronics and Radio Engineering Limited, which explained the 70-foot aerial array that stood alongside the main house. The house was genuine Georgian and well preserved. Once a year the village fete was held in the grounds, and the chairman of the Rural District Council never failed to congratulate the directors in public for their preservation of "one of England's truly stately homes." It was accepted by the locals that they were never invited inside because of all the valuable antique furniture.

Inside, the house was lined with reinforced concrete and a network of elaborate wiring. It was the headquarters and operational center of SIS—Secret Intelligence Service—a title rather resented by MI-5 as it seemed to imply that others were publicity seekers. The resentment was no more than, say, between the CID and the uniformed police.

The meeting was in the luxurious boardroom and was between the Prime Minister and the Director of Operations SIS. After some preliminary chitchat the PM said, "Well, Sir John, I gather you want to consult me about some problem."

"Prime Minister, we have a very urgent problem.

24

I'd better fill in some of the background for you, and first of all, I must inform you that none of your predecessors after Sir Winston were apprised of this information."

The PM raised the well-known eyebrows, and the Director hurried on with his discourse before he could be questioned.

"Instructions were given to us to that effect by Sir Winston himself, and we understand that Mr. Roosevelt and the Canadian Prime Minister acted similarly in their countries—the matter goes back to the summer of 1940."

The PM made no move to interrupt now. He looked serious and concerned as Sir John continued.

"The War Office had passed information concerning the Nazi Operation Sea Lion to the Pentagon and other allied or friendly governments as a matter of routine. It seems that this caused, or led to, a meeting in private in August 1940 of the President and the Canadian Prime Minister. At this conference it was decided that in the event of Operation Sea Lion being successful —in other words, the successful occupation of part of Britain by the Germans—the planned transfer of the British Government to Canadian soil would not in fact be allowed by the Canadian Government. Furthermore, both the American and Canadian Heads of State informed Sir Winston that in the event of a German occupation they would both accept the status quo and arrange some form of accommodation with the Third Reich."

The Prime Minister was silent for several minutes. "That would have been the end for all of us—for all of Europe, in fact."

"I'm afraid so, sir. Here only Sir Winston knew of this decision. It was given him in person by a special aide from the White House and the Governor-General. Altogether only a handful of people knew of the meeting and the decision."

"What was going to happen to the Royals?"

25

"They were to be allowed to go to Canada, as would the other Royals in exile and the leading politicians, whose lives would be in danger. These included Sir Winston, of course."

"What did Sir Winston say to all that?"

"I understand he was ill in bed for two days and that was that." He waited patiently for the PM to absorb the ramifications of this information. It had taken him days to get it out of his mind when he had first heard the story. Even now he found it frightening to think what it must have meant at the time that it happened.

The PM sighed. "Well, thank God it never happened." He looked expectantly at Sir John.

"That's why I needed to see you here, sir, because it's possible that it could all come out—be made public. The Americans have just helped us break a rather complex code, and although we only have part of the message it looks as if there will be a definite attempt to publish the information, including photostats of the minutes of that meeting and of the personal letters to Churchill from Roosevelt and Mackenzie King."

"To what end?"

"Well, our first evaluation indicated that it was another piece of spite by the French—the decoded instructions make it clear that the French are involved. But they also show that the Poles are in it too, probably controlling the operation. The embarrassment to the Americans would go down well in France, and although de Gaulle is dead just think back to his 'Vive le Québec libre' speech when he was visiting Trudeau. They'd enjoy stirring up the Canadians, and the French-Canadians wouldn't let it alone; they'd get a lot of political mileage out of it."

"There'd be plenty of willing hands to stir the pot here too," the PM interjected.

"Precisely. Well, we reckoned the French could do

this on their own, so we did an extended evaluation on possible reasons for the Poles' involvement, and our conclusion is that this is going to be a big operation and the French bit is only the beginning. The Poles, or the KGB through the Poles, are going to use the resentment against the Americans and Canadians to get them out of Europe. This is going to be an operation to bust up NATO—to finish once and for all any American involvement in Europe. You've seen the current situation report on the Warsaw Pact and NATO strengths."

The PM nodded but he didn't speak. He was imagining the newspaper headlines. He could write them himself. "USA Ratted on Allies," "Roosevelt Planned Hitler Deal," "Europe Sold Out by Americans." There would be double-page spreads in the Sunday *Times* and the *Observer*, long discussions on TV, every American-hater in Europe would have a field day, and no European government would be able to control the revulsion against the United States. The Americans would be glad to be squeezed out of NATO. They could escape from European commitments which they already saw as another potential Vietnam. And not a voice would be raised against their withdrawal, from either side of the Atlantic. The Russians would use their contacts in Europe and keep the pot boiling for a year without making even a comment in public. Even the UN would be a bigger shambles than it already was.

He looked over at his companion. "The evaluation you mentioned. Was that the one that included the film of the Russian exercise called Dnieper and our exercise Strong Express?"

"Yes, Prime Minister. If I can remind you it showed that even with the Americans heavily involved in NATO we are already completely outgunned and outmanned. In fact, the differential is three to one in every area except nuclear subs. If the Warsaw Pact countries made a move against NATO today they could be at the Channel ports in three days at the outside. Only American involvement in NATO keeps them out. With the Americans back in the States I'm not sure the Soviets need take much aggressive action; every government in Europe would be doing its own deal—quick."

The PM didn't like nonpoliticians telling him what governments would or would not do, but he knew all too well that SIS knew more about politicians than they did themselves. He stood up. "What do you want to do? I suppose D notices today to the newspapers."

"I'd suggest not, sir—not yet, anyway. A lot of them won't even know what it's all about, and they'll feel that if it's worth censoring it's worth investigating. The President has kept it under wraps, and they've everything to lose if it breaks over there. I'd be grateful if you kept an ear open with the newspaper proprietors. There'll probably be a hefty fee demanded for this stuff, and that generally means proprietor's approval first. Then we come to the question of the French Government. I'd be surprised if they were involved—officially, anyway—but we can't ignore that they've been playing footsie with the Soviets for over a year now. I think it's more likely that they know something's going on and are turning a blind eye."

He pushed across the silver box of cigarettes to the Prime Minister, who shook his head as Sir John continued.

"I'd like to suggest, sir, that I put one man alone onto this. He can have all the resources he wants, but he and I will be the only ones who know what it's all about. I'd also like to suggest that this meeting has officially never taken place. For those who need to know, I suggest we say we were discussing Operation Ice-Eyes."

"How is that going, by the way?"

"Very slowly, sir. Under control but we're not rushing it."

As the Prime Minister had his hand on the big brass doorknob, he said, "If you get these people, we're still going to have problems at the Old Bailey. Her Majesty's Judges are pretty touchy at the number of in-camera cases they're getting these days."

"This isn't going to come to court, sir, we shall see to that. They'd use a trial to spill the beans. It would suit their book very well. Any man involved will be dealt with—but the first thing is the documents. Without those no paper anywhere in the world would print, and if they did nobody'd believe them. There'll be no talkers when we've finished, sir."

They exchanged a brief glance, but the Director didn't elaborate. They both knew what he meant.

There was a long piece in *L'Humanité* the next day about the outrageous behavior of the British Secret Service in forcibly abducting a member of the staff of the Polish liner *Batory* and then hiding their savage assault behind the outrageous suggestion that a Polish citizen had requested political asylum. There was a much smaller, less raucous piece in *Le Figaro*, and nothing in *Le Monde*.

Sir John Walker, Director of Operations SIS, opened the file from his archive section. The first piece of paper was the translation of an extract from the speech made by Hitler to the Reichstag on the evening of July 19, 1940.

"From Britain," he had said, "I now hear only a single cry—not of the people but of the politicians—that the war must go on! I do not know whether these politicians already have a correct idea of what the continuation of this struggle will be like. They do, it is true, declare that they will carry on with the war and that, even if Great Britain should perish, they would carry on from Canada. I can hardly believe that they mean by this that

29

the people of Britain are to go to Canada. Presumably only those gentlemen interested in the continuation of their war will go there. The people, I am afraid, will have to remain in Britain and . . . will certainly regard the war with other eyes than their so-called leaders in Canada.

"Believe me, gentlemen, I feel a deep disgust for this type of unscrupulous politician who wrecks whole nations. It almost causes me pain to think that I should have been selected by fate to deal the final blow to the structure which these men have already set tottering. . . . Mr. Churchill . . . no doubt will already be in Canada, where the money and children of those principally interested in the war have already been sent. Mr. Churchill ought perhaps, for once, to believe me when I prophesy that a great Empire will be destroyed—an Empire which it was never my intention to destroy or even to harm. . . ."

4

WHEN SIR JOHN WALKER had finished briefing Anders, he said, "How do you feel about taking it on, Major?"

Anders stood up and looked out of the window. "Oh, I'll take it on, sir. There's not much to go on, but we've got the defecting Pole and the text of the microfilm. I'll be glad when I can pick up a lead to the Frenchmen. Is Farrow still in Berlin?"

"Yes, he's there for another seven months."

"How do you want me to report?"

"At least daily, but don't hesitate to contact me if you want more bodies. As long as you don't give any indication of what you're after, there's no reason why you shouldn't use all resources." He was shuffling papers on his desk when he looked up and said quietly, "I don't want any of these men around afterwards, Anders— you understand that."

Anders nodded.

Ten minutes later he was on the Portsmouth road heading for London and Zygmund Kujawski.

When Kujawski discovered that he'd lost the two coins he had panicked. He had just wanted any refuge that was going, but now he was out of danger he felt lonely and frightened. He wasn't a bad cook; maybe he'd get employment with one of the Polish cafés in Fulham or Soho. When the British gave him his freedom and temporary identity papers, insurance cards, and £100 he was sorely tempted to pay another visit to the blonde in Soho. But on second thought he decided he'd better not go there again.

It was raining when he left Wormwood Scrubs, and he called a taxi whose driver had stopped for a smoke. He'd swung the door to before he saw the man sitting on the back seat. His hand went back to the door handle and then dropped as he saw the gun pointing at him.

The big man said *"Siadaj,"* and Kujawski obediently sat. The driver seemed to know where they were going.

"Where are you taking me? Who are you?" Kujawski said. All he got was a dirty look.

After about twenty minutes the taxi stopped and the driver opened two big wooden gates and they drove down a slope and stopped again. Kujawski could just make out a rambling building with a door marked Studio Jason. The big man gave him a dig with the gun and he stepped down. The driver opened the door and there was a flood of light. They walked down a corridor. Through an open door, Kujawski could see films hanging from lines, drying over the sinks. And then they were in a small room with cone-shaped blocks covering all the walls and ceilings. Kujawski had seen such a room only once before in his life, at the Moscow Center on Kuznetsky Most, and he knew what it was for. Anechoic chambers are great for hi-fi recordings—and keeping screams from the outside world. There was a heavy wooden chair in the center of the room, and the big man waved him to it and nodded to the driver, who closed the door and left.

The big man sat on a chair near him. "Now, Kujawski, let's get down to it. I warn you, you can have it the easy way or the rough way. It's all the same to me."

"Who are you? You speak in Polish, are you a Pole?"

"Right now, who do you work for?"

"Ministry of the Interior."

"Oh, for God's sake, who do you work for, who's your boss?"

"Antoni Shirilov."

The big man laughed. Shirilov's men were the dregs. Even the KGB called them *shavki*, stray dogs that sniff around dustbins. "Where were you trained?"

"Warsaw and then the Moscow Center."

"Which bit of the Moscow Center, Dzerzhinski Street or at Kuznetsky Most?"

"Kuznetsky Most."

"When?"

"Six months ago."

"For this mission?"

"Partly."

"OK. Tell me about this mission."

Then Anders got the story of the special coins. One to be planted in Kensington Gardens taped to a metal flower tag and one to be paid to a tobacconist in Archer Street after asking for a packet of Gauloises and refusing to pay more. Just a low-grade courier, a dead-letter box and a post office. During the interrogation Anders learned that there were three separate apparats in London, all controlled by a resident who was unknown to Kujawski. But he knew that his apparat had connections in Paris. He'd been instructed to drop the coins, go to Paris, telephone Kléber 9047, and ask for Monsieur Québec, who would give him instructions.

Anders took several photographs of Kujawski and then said, "All right, Kujawski, you've been a good boy. I'll give you a rest. Which do you prefer, tea or coffee?"

"Tea."

"With milk?"

"No, just lemon."

Anders smoked a cigarette while the Pole drank the

33

tea. He wasn't moved when Kujawski's head went back and the choking started. It never took more than a couple of minutes, and if you've got to die this is one of the quickest and easiest ways because the central nervous system is paralyzed in seconds.

There was a burial next day in a special section of the cemetery near Kew Gardens, but no mourners. Just Major Anders and the taxi driver. It was barely light, but there was no rain and the soil was loose down to the clay.

Tadeusz Anders was a Northumbrian, born in Morpeth in 1941. His father was a cavalry officer in one of the crack Polish cavalry regiments, captured by the Germans on the second of September, 1939. Three months later he was an officer in the Free Polish Army. He'd fallen in love in a matter of weeks with an English girl, and his good looks and old-world charm had made her one of the many Easter brides the next year. Tadeusz was born the following spring. His father had died in the assault on Monte Cassino, and young Anders was absorbed into the general pattern of life in the pleasant little town. He was taught Polish and Russian at the little Polish school that the Polish colony ran on weekends, and he was thought well of by both the Polish and English communities. The life in Northumberland was not unlike life in small Polish towns, and the wild sweeping vistas of the countryside were explored with other boys and girls. His mother was happy, working as a teacher at the primary school, and young Tadeusz was obviously the apple of her eye. She didn't spoil him, but she cared about the boy as if he were husband as well as son.

In the summer after his eighteenth birthday they heard that he'd been awarded a place at the university.

Two days later his mother came home a little late, and when they were having their evening meal she told the boy that she was going to marry a farmer from the Alnwick area. She explained that it would never make any difference to them; they'd always be the same.

The wedding was a few weeks later, and Tadeusz was to stay with an aunt while the couple had a brief honeymoon in Edinburgh. There were many people at the wedding—she was loved and respected—and when Tadeusz stood with the others waving good-bye he too saw the tears in her eyes, but he couldn't bear that she was smiling too. And her new husband had his arm around her.

Everything he had went into the old army kit bag, including his father's medals from the small glass-fronted showcase. He went down to London the same day, and two days later he was starting his recruit training at Caterham barracks, saying "Yes, trained soldier" and "No, trained soldier" to his three-month seniors in the Coldstream Guards. He had remembered a sign on the Great North Road just a few miles from Morpeth. It said COLDSTREAM 22 MILES. He didn't reveal his true name and age until he was commissioned.

In some ways the army is a quite kindly orphanage, and it liked the courage and ability of the young lieutenant who absorbed so readily all they had to teach him. Because of the Russian and Polish he was transferred to the Intelligence Corps, and by the usual process of ups and downs he became one of the more experienced and valued officers in SIS. "Singleness of purpose" was the phrase most often used by his various superiors. He never saw or heard of his mother again. He never talked about his childhood and almost succeeded in never thinking about it. He felt he'd learned a lesson about women from his mother, and he was glad he'd learned it early. No woman would ever again get the chance to bring back that sudden cold that gripped his limbs, the feeling of darkness and wind. The feeling that the lights have all gone out. Loneliness.

He was well liked by men and women. Despite his looks, his vitality, and his obvious intelligence, for some reason men never saw him as a rival. For the same reasons, many young women saw him as a husband, but none saw him as a lover.

At nine thirty Anders was in Commander Bryant's office at New Scotland Yard and Bryant was reading aloud bits from the post-mortem report on Ethel Bates.

"Cause of death, strangulation—the wound to the chest and abdomen was inflicted after death." He looked over at Anders. "Typical action of a criminal psychopath, although they generally inflict lots of small wounds. This guy had done this before, I reckon; the knife only stopped when it hit the pelvic bridge. Victim had had sexual intercourse within two hours of death—had not eaten for approximately six hours—had had a child at about age twenty—and the rest's just minor bits and pieces, usual stuff about dyed hair and hammertoes."

"Fingerprints or anything else?"

"Well, that's quite interesting. In a dump like that you've got a number of visitors. We traced nine different sets apart from the girl's."

"Any identified?"

"Yes, three sets. One was a Detective Constable Lovejoy, the second a Mrs. Palmer, an old biddy who came in for an hour a day to tidy up—probably took calls from clients when the girl was out—and the last lot was from a known criminal by the name of Red Levi."

"Why Red? Has he got red hair or something?"

Bryant smiled. "I gather from the local police it's nothing to do with his appearance but his sporting interests. It seems that on two recent occasions when Moscow

Dynamo played over here he was heard shouting for them. Somebody gave him the nickname and it stuck."

Anders seemed lost in his thoughts; then he surfaced. "Can I have photostats of all of it?"

"Yes, I've had copies done for you. Call me again if I can help you in any way."

Anders was sitting in one of the back offices of Albany Street police station reading through the file on Valentin Levi. Both parents had emigrated from Odessa in 1919. Their only son was born in Whitechapel, London, 1925. He had convictions for petty larceny, breaking and entering, and being in possession of goods knowing them to be stolen. No crimes of violence. Anders noted the known addresses and associates.

Krezki had told His Excellency that morning that he would be away from his chauffeuring duties for some weeks. It was all very nice having a cover, especially when it allowed diplomatic immunity to be claimed, but the duties of being an agent were too time-consuming to double up once an operation had started.

Chelsea was playing Aston Villa in a cup replay, and although there were still ten minutes to go the crowds were already leaving. It was 1 to 1 and it looked all set for yet another replay. Krezki left with the stream and walked back over the bridge and turned right, down into King's Road past the junk shops, and ten minutes later he was back in his room.

He hadn't been wasting time at the football match, because although he had to send a message to Moscow, he needed the night because a dark signal path gave his signal more strength. It had cost the funds £150 to get the coin, and it was obvious that he'd still only got half the message. He could contact the Frenchmen but he needed the rest of the instructions. Levi could be useful in the future. He'd done this job quickly and efficiently.

He unscrewed the cabinet from the bathroom wall and eased out the six loose bricks. The transmitter was quite small but it needed 75 feet of aerial and he'd had to wind this around and around in the loft. The encoding took over an hour, and then he used the Morse key into the tape recorder. When it was all taped he played it back twice to check. He recorded at fifteen inches per second and then switched on the small, very high-speed recorder. The whole message only took nine seconds at its final speed and was just a squiggle of sounds. Any British radio monitors would have only those nine seconds to get the necessary two different fixes to locate his transmitter. He plugged the tape recorder into the socket on the transmitter, waited ten minutes, and on the last bleep of the BBC's time signal for the nine o'clock news he pressed the key down for thirty seconds and that was that. By the time he had the radio back in its hiding place the news bulletin was almost over, but he turned on the small transistor radio in the big room.

When the football results were read out he was surprised to hear that Chelsea had won 2 to 1 with a goal by Osgood two minutes from the end. He went out and bought an *Evening Standard,* and feeling rather pleased with life he went in for a drink at the local, reading the back-page account of the match while he sipped a large whisky. When he laid the paper down on the table it was nearly ten minutes before he noticed the screaming headlines on the front page: Maniac Sex Killer Strikes in Soho! And there followed the story of Ethel Bates, and Krezki felt very cold despite the Saturday-night haze in the pub. The piece ended with a warning from the deputy head of the Murder Squad and an assurance that the maniac concerned would be hunted down as a matter of urgency.

5

THERE WAS ONLY a single yellow line in Soho Lane but it was a narrow street, and although it was one way there was barely room for two cars abreast. Police Constable Evans saw the parked taxi just below the Lotus Strip Club and sharpened his pace. The taxi's time flag was down; it was probably waiting for one of the strippers doing the rounds from club to club. There was an American Ford Mustang trying to ease past the taxi. It had one of those fancy horns that was playing Jeremiah Clark's "Trumpet Voluntary" or some damn thing. It was all the taxi driver's fault, but PC Evans took the Mustang driver's name and address just for the hell of it and cautioned him about using an illegal car horn. When he'd finished, the taxi was still there so he kept his notebook open.

"You know it's an offense to wait on a yellow line, driver—you've been here five minutes or more to my knowledge—so let's be having you. I'll have your license first." And he put his hand on the open window frame.

The cabbie reached to his inside pocket, pulled out his wallet, and, opening it, said, "Don't take all night reading it, mate."

PC Evans had seen a similar card on his training course, but he'd never seen a real one before. He wasn't even sure what SIS was, but he knew you left them alone.

He nodded and folded up his notebook and was

about to turn away when the driver said, "Don't put it away, mate, write something down—any bloody thing— or they'll think I'm waiting for the Queen or something."

He took the point and wrote down carefully his own name and address. Then he walked on toward Shaftesbury Avenue.

Inside the Lotus there was a good Saturday-night crowd. Ethel's death was three days old now and its first impact was over. Life, like show biz, carried on. Red Levi hadn't been to a strip show before and reckoned he'd been missing out. It wasn't what he'd expected. He knew they took all their clothes off, but for the life of him he couldn't see why they took such a time. The blonde who was on now was great, but she must have taken five minutes just to get her bra off. God help ·'em if they're ever late for work, he thought. She was down to her pants, one hand swinging some old-fashioned beads and the other tentatively, slowly, pushing down one side of the white cotton briefs millimeter by millimeter.

"Bloody stupid," he said to the man standing next to him. "Why don't she use both hands? Takes bloody hours and you can't see her knockers for those bleeding beads. Bloody deliberate, if you ask me."

Some of the cognoscenti hissed him to be quiet as if he'd clapped between movements at a Mozart performance by the Amadeus. But time passed and eventually the pants came off, and as the young blonde twirled them around to emphasize her victorious struggle there were two seconds of complete silence except for the canned music. The lights wobbled, went out, and by popular request came on again and there she was. But Levi was incensed. "Why's the silly bitch standing with her legs crossed?" he said, turning to find support from the man next to him. Then he gasped. "Hey, that's hurting my back," and as he said it he saw the look in the big man's eyes. They were as cold as a Moscow street.

"Don't make a fuss, Levi, or you'll get it now. Turn round and come with me."

His mouth trembled. "What you want, guv? You a copper?"

The gun just pressed harder into his kidneys. The taxi took them down to the back street in Pimlico and the room with the cones on the wall.

When the big man spoke in Russian, Levi knew it was trouble.

"Levi, I'm in a hurry. What did you do with the coin?"

"Are you one of them?"

"One of what?"

"Well, you know—whatever that Pole does."

"What Pole?"

Levi fell silent. He'd forgotten about the girl till the big man had taken him away. But the big man wasn't a copper. No matter what they said in the papers, a copper'd never dare go on like this chap. And he obviously knew about the 10p piece. Levi had guessed the Pole was up to no good or he wouldn't have paid so much to get just one coin back. Especially a dud one. Maybe this chap was the girl's boy friend or brother or something. Then the big fist crashed into the side of Levi's face and he cried out, "For Christ's sake, what d'ye want from me?"

"The Pole's name."

"I don't know his bloody name, mate. They all sound the same to me. All I know is he's a Pole and he lives down Chelsea or Fulham."

"Where, exactly?"

"I don't know. We met in this pub."

"Which pub?"

"It's called the Bricklayer's Arms—between Fulham Road and King's Road."

"Is that where he first contacted you?"

"No, he came up to me in Berwick Street Market."

"And fixed for you to steal the coin."

"It wasn't stealing, guv. It was 'is or so 'e said."

"How much did he pay you?"

"Hundred quid."

"Did he tell you to kill the girl?"

Levi was holding his face and his lower jaw was trembling. "No, I done that. I don't know why, it just come over me—seemed all wrong, her letting an old sod like me have it—and she laughed about it and—"

"Forget it. What did you do with the coin?"

"I give it to the Pole and 'e give me the other fifty quid. Wouldn't even stay for a drink wiv me."

"Did you open the coin?"

"I tried but I couldn't; it was too tight. You'd 'ave needed a knife. The Pole opened it, though, before he give me the money. There was a piece of plastic inside."

Anders sat absorbing the information and thinking, and after a time Levi said tentatively, "You goin' to turn me in, guv'nor?"

Anders went back over Levi's answers to check if there was anything missing. "How did he know about you?"

"I think he must 'ave asked somebody in the market. Prob'ly said he wanted something nicked." He shrugged. "They all know me."

After he'd finished reporting to the Director of Operations SIS, Anders said, "Do you want me to hand Levi over to the police or not?"

There was a long silence. "That's quite a problem. I'll leave it to your discretion." And then Sir John had hung up.

Anders knew that when they left these sorts of things "to your discretion" it meant they couldn't bring themselves to say out loud what they really wanted. Probably caused by sitting in offices all day. But he'd got the message. There were good reasons for disposing of Levi. He was a criminal, psycho, a murderer, and the murder of the girl would bring out all the rest if it went to trial. But Anders wasn't sure. He'd give it a day or so.

6

THE TRIDENT was bouncing a bit in the head winds and the loudspeaker said, "Please fasten your seat belts. We shall shortly be landing at Orly International Airport. We shall be landing at approximately seventeen thirty-five, fifteen minutes behind schedule. The Met report gives seasonal average temperatures and showers. Thank you."

Anders took a taxi into Paris and asked the driver to drop him at the Ritz, where he had a whisky and made a telephone call. Then he took his small bag, walked to the far corner of the Place Vendôme, and a few minutes later was checking in at a small hotel in the Boulevard des Capucines.

He was just finishing his bath when the phone rang. *"Monsieur Macdonald vous attends au bar, m'sieu."*

Anders asked them to send him up. He was looking forward to seeing Mac again; it had been over a year now. They were having their second drink when Anders said, "Did you check on the Kléber phone number I got from Kujawski?"

Bill Macdonald nodded. "Aye, it's a transit house the Russian Embassy runs. Supposed to be for VIPs staying more than two days. It's a house in Avenue Foch—nice villa in its own grounds. Bags of security, guards,

44

dogs, and I'd guess a lot of electronics." He grinned. "In short, a hidey-hole for the KGB."

"Any idea of the staff?"

"It ebbs and flows but there are a few old hands. We've got some access there through SMERT."

"Is that Okolovich's old lot?"

"That's it. At the moment they've got the only really effective penetration of the Soviet system. They won't carry out operational missions for us any more, but they cooperate from time to time. They need the dough."

"How soon can you contact your guy inside the house?"

"Not till tomorrow noon."

"OK. Tell him I shall be phoning that Kléber number at exactly 4 P.M. Ask him to check on the guy who handles the call and give us a rundown on his background."

Anders enjoyed the performance of *Les Pêcheurs de Perles*. The aria for two tenors was wonderful music, strongly masculine and very much to his taste. He made a bit of a pig of himself with asparagus after the show. He couldn't stick the English stuff, all green and thin. This was Dutch, and the thick white stalks were succulent and sweet. He'd take a walk and then read in bed. He was looking forward to reading the latest copy of *Voyenwa Mysl*, available only to professional officers of the Soviet Armed Forces—and, of course, SIS, CIA, and all the other private armies.

As he walked back across the bridge over the Seine it started to rain. A mounted policeman trotted by, and the rhythm of the horse's hoofs on the cobbles suddenly put the clock back for him, and he heard his mother's voice saying a little Polish nursery rhyme: "*Jedzie, jedzie, pan, pan. Na koniku sam sam.*" Then it was gone, no more than a flicker of summer lightning.

He shivered involuntarily and realized how tired he was and hurried back to the hotel.

The phone call to the Kléber number was short and in French. Anders was given seven addresses and told to pass them to the Frenchmen as laid down in his instructions from Moscow and to give them any help they required and report by telephone to Paris on even dates.

The news from Mac's informant was scant. The man who had handled the phone call was Polish. A junior officer in Z-11 and a specialist in explosives, he had been at the Paris house only for five weeks. Didn't appear to be very busy.

Anders phoned the stately home in Hampshire to get a check on the addresses and got their report just after midnight. Two were the U.S. Embassy and the U.S. Information Office in London; the five others were Canada House and the London headquarters of large Canadian companies. Mac was still with him when the report came through, and it was clear enough what it all added up to. It wasn't going to be just the documents.

He was silent while he drank his vodka. When he put the glass down, he said, "Mac, have you got a chap I could borrow who knows his way around the Gaullists and maybe knows the rough boys?"

"Which particular rough boys? There's a lot of them in Paris these days."

"Political rough boys, the *barbouze* types, ex-army people, ex-resistance types still in the racket."

"That's not going to be easy. I certainly haven't got anyone who moves in all those circles—and if I had I wouldn't lend him anyway. I might dredge up somebody who knows the dope but isn't actually in on the action. Would that do?"

"Maybe, but he'd have to be an experienced operator."

"I'll call you tomorrow when I've checked my records."

Anders was shaving when his doorbell buzzed the next morning and he shouted "Come in" and then remembered that the door was locked. When he opened the door, the girl said, "Hello, Tad."

"Who are you?"

"A friend of yours sent me. May I come in?"

His phone rang and he hesitated; then he showed the girl into the sitting room, closed the door, and picked up the phone. It was Mac. "Tad, I'm sending you a girl."

"She's just arrived—this minute."

"She's what you want. I'd forgotten about her. I couldn't use her over here, she's blown. She's brought some of my notes about herself with her. Just as a double check I've given her a password—you say a couple of words from the "Marseillaise" and she'll go on from there. She's experienced, bright, and plenty of guts. Let me know if you take her, and if you do she'd better be on your account for pay and rations."

Anders completed his shave, finished dressing, and tried to sort out his thoughts. He didn't want a woman on the job, but it looked as if this girl was all he'd get from Paris SIS. He walked into the sitting room, sat down opposite the girl, and said, *"Qu'un sang impur—"*

She frowned for a moment, then laughed. *"Abreuve nos sillons."*

Anders had never been sure about the difference between "beautiful" and "pretty." They were one of those odd but common parasynonyms that the English language enjoys as a result of such a wealth of adjectives for every noun. It made English an imprecise language, but it was surely why the poetry was so good. But there *was* an English word for this girl, a glowing orange word

47

like a big, round, golden autumn moon or the gloss on a racehorse's neck. She was gorgeous: tall, perfect features, and a face that was alive. She was wearing a black suit with black braiding on the edges and a plain white silk blouse. Although he wasn't an expert on such matters, he guessed from what he saw that she was wearing nylon stockings on the long shapely legs. She was smiling. The white, even teeth were made for eating apples.

She held out an envelope and he took it. "I'm sorry. Would you like a drink?"

She shook her head, and the long blond hair bounced like a TV shampoo ad. "No, thanks, but I'd love a cigarette." As she leaned back and exhaled the first smoke he opened the envelope. There were two pages of typing.

She was Marie-Claire Foubert, age twenty-seven. Daughter of Jean Foubert, an officer in the Chasseurs Alpins and then in Special Operations Executive, captured in Perpignan by the Milice in 1944 and handed over to the Gestapo. Died in Fresnes prison two weeks later. Mother, Seychelloise from the main island of Mahé. Now remarried to an official of the Malagasy Republic and living in Diego Suarez.

The girl had trained as a journalist and was now a free lance, also doing odd bits of research for other journalists.

She'd been recruited into SIS when she was twenty and had not been used for the past year. Her last pistol shooting was 97s at 25 meters, and she had had full unarmed-combat training. Languages—French, English, and German. No police or security prosecutions. Had been expected to marry an Englishman, a member of SIS killed in Berlin eighteen months ago, running a network into the East German Republic. Emotionally stable, health A-1. Receiving small pension from SIS. Not to be used in Metropolitan France, Algeria, Saigon, or Thailand. Appendix scar and a series of burn scars on upper left arm and shoulder. Educated at the lycée at Lyons and the Sorbonne. Had failed radio training. Had undergone an abortion in London at age twenty-five following multi-rape while held in military jail No. 7 Saigon. Had numbered account in Zurich Landesbank No. 4937212. Subject not aware that this bank account known to SIS. Account approximately $57,000 at most recent check (fifteen days lapsed time). Also deposit and current accounts in the Banque d'Indochine, 30,000 and 278 new francs respectively. Present associates—journalists, broadcasters. Politics—none. No known close relationships at time of report. Only child. Father's relations had severed connections on marriage.

When he'd finished reading, Anders looked across at the girl and for a few moments enjoyed looking at her face.

"Did Mac give you any idea what I want you for?"

She shook her head. "No. He said only you were SIS."

"Apart from the areas that are prohibited to you, is there any kind of work that you dislike?"

"You mean SIS work?" He nodded and she shrugged and said, "No, I've covered a fair range for them. Can you tell me what this operation's about?"

"It's better if you don't know—at this stage, anyway. I'm not sure myself how you can help, but there's a group of Frenchmen in London that I need penetrating. I think you could help there."

Two hours later they were in widely separated seats on the midevening flight to London. An American in the next seat to the girl was doing a fast line. It was Anders' impression that the American was doing well.

7

AT THE BOTTOM of the Rue Mouffetard there is a lively market, and there you can buy, if you can't afford better, the basics of wines and food, clothes, and hardware. Its name, derived from "skunk," once reflected the stench of skinners and tanners; now it is the smell of rotting vegetables, putrid fish, and at night the acrid reek of urine. But if you walk up the hill, the Rue Mouffetard becomes the Rue Descartes. Nobody knows why it is called the Rue Descartes, because its eponymous hero lived some streets away in the Rue Rollin whenever he left his home in Holland. And the crooked, eccentric little street bears no relation to the planned and orderly tastes of the *philosophe*. When you near the top you can see a bell tower, and beneath it is the Lycée Henri IV. The students at the lycée mainly arrive at the bus stop or the Métro station on the Rue Monge. And behind the walls of the lycée the young French write the penetrating analyses of the arts and sciences dictated by their teachers. It's a rigid system, so if on some Friday afternoon you were able to visit the lycées in London, Madrid, Lyons, or Rome, all the red notebooks would be filling up with the same words on the same subject. At a lycée you're there to learn; the thinking can come later.

In 1949 one of the pupils at the lycée in the Rue Descartes was André Prouvost. He didn't come by Métro or by bus, he walked. And that was the root of the trouble. He walked because his family lived in three rooms in the Rue Mouffetard itself. Which meant he was condescended to by the cool sons and daughters of Parisian merchants and minor Catholic ambassadors. He made it to the Sorbonne but he never forgot the lycée.

Because he was bright rather than intelligent, it was easier to add his personal anger to some more established and traditional protest. Such martyrs always need extremes, so it had to be far left or far right. He should have chosen the left because he was a born destroyer, not a builder, but at the time to choose we are often influenced by chance, like small-boat sailors mistaking an offshore puff for a prevailing wind.

As is so often the case with young men, André Prouvost's offshore zephyr was a girl, the lively, pretty daughter of a member of the Assembly—a Republican, for they'd not yet needed to use the qualifying "Gaullist." From the lively daughter he'd learned the excitement of breasts and thighs, and from the livelier father he'd heard of life in the Free French with de Gaulle, in London and Algiers. Like a child rolling together two pieces of Plasticine he'd merged his insults at the lycée with the insults to the General from Colombey-les-Deux-Eglises. A hatred for the English and the Americans was a natural consequence and was no hindrance to any career that depended even slightly on the establishment and its patronage. There had been many small jobs, but he finally found his niche as editor of a monthly called *Les Maquisards* which kept alive the history of the Maquis and other groups of the Resistance. It was not easy to omit the contributions of the Communists and the English, but it could be done. And Prouvost did it. As time went by he was useful to various government agencies, acting as an informer for the *barbouzes* dealing with student riots and, on occasion, flattered by a call from the Deuxième Bureau. He wrote as a free lance for sev-

51

eral Paris papers and magazines whenever an acid pen might please the President or usefully needle the Americans. When others were planning *Opération boule de neige*, André Prouvost was an obvious recruit.

Route Nationale 9 sweeps down southward, following the Mediterranean coast from Béziers, through Narbonne to Perpignan and the Spanish border. You wouldn't find your way around Perpignan now with a 1941 street guide. The Quai de Lattre-de-Tassigny, Avenue Général Leclerc, Avenue de la Grande Bretagne, and especially la Place de la Résistance all had other names then. Today there are two good wide roads leading to the Spanish frontier, but in 1941 there was only one, and it wasn't good and it wasn't wide. But in 1941 there were people in London who said that that little road from Perpignan was more important than the Champs-Elysées. If your Special Operations Executive network had been broken up and you had to disappear, or you were shot-down air crew, then Perpignan was where you headed for.

There was a well-organized chain to get you over the Pyrenees, and when you crossed into Spain, if you were exceptionally lucky, you made it down to Madrid and the British Embassy did the rest. If you weren't quite so lucky you went into Camp Miranda; you'd still get to London but it took much longer. From time to time the Nazis put one of their own into the chain. They made sure that he took the same time to get to London, and he too ended up with all the others in the Royal Victoria Patriotic School in Wandsworth. The RVPS was the most expert interrogation center in the UK and it was there that they carefully and patiently took you and your story apart and sewed it all together again. No German plants got through, because whether it was the Abwehr or the Gestapo they were always too thorough and too German. They knew exactly what was paid to the shepherds and smugglers who took the wandering boys up the mountain, but they never actually went, so they never discovered the missing bit. Everybody paid the going rate, in cash, before starting out; it might have been wartime, the guides patriots, but it was a trade and only a tidy German mind wouldn't have realized that you'd get stuck for another 2,000 francs just short of the top of the mountains. IOUs on the British Government were sometimes accepted, and they all eventually got paid.

Many of the wanderers were in hiding in the town for weeks before a guide could be arranged, and one of the hiding places was a family butcher's in a small street near the Citadelle. The son of the house had never been in the army. He had a murmur of the heart, as the doctors put it. It sounded romantic but it wasn't. He risked his life for four and a half years, and in 1946 Pierre Firette went to Paris to the Elysée Palace and shook hands with the General and collected his Légion d'Honneur. An MBE came some months after. When he had read the extracts from the President's memoirs in *Paris Match* and seen how Churchill and Roosevelt had treated the leader of Free France, he'd sent it back to the British Embassy in disgust.

He married a local girl in 1949. There were fortunately no children for she turned out to be a shrew, which had its consolations. Glad to be away from her, he had time to develop other talents. He was *boule* champion for the Grands Pyrénées and so deeply involved in politics that it necessitated frequent trips to Paris. It was his enthusiasm and singlemindedness in these circles that eventually led him to the London Hilton.

For those who loved prewar Paris with real love, it needed no touchstone. It could be the "Madeleine" or Fauré's "Requiem" that worked the magic button, or just Josephine Baker singing "J'ai deux amours."

For those who now find it hard and shoddy, its inhabitants greedy and without love, there is, some say, a way to recall the magic, and once more injected maybe the love will feed and grow. At the side of the Tuileries Gardens you'll find they've reopened La Musée de l'Orangerie. Walk through, ignoring the Modiglianis, the Renoirs, and even the Cézannes, because the cure is not art. There are two oval rooms with eight of Monet's "Nymphea" studies. People stand silent in the sea of whiteness, and the simple arches are a balm to frozen hearts. The paintings are not what matters, only the thought that put them in those gentle rooms, in that pellucid light. It's a place to believe in God, a place to fall in love, a place to wash the mind. And every Sunday, almost without fail, Paul Loussier went there with his young wife. At fifty he hadn't won. What he was good at held no interest for him; he wanted something else, something heroic, something decisive. What he was good at was civil engineering, and there had been a time when the sweeping spans of a bridge could bring delight. But that seemed long ago: another marriage, another life, another world. A single sunny year before the war and then the years of gray destruction, when a patriotic Frenchman helped foreigners to blow up French bridges and mine viaducts to stop the Nazis bringing up their troops. When that time was all over the grayness still didn't go. He designed 170 kilometers of new Routes Nationales with overpasses and bridges, lighting and landscaping, but the magic wasn't there.

Paul Loussier had been an active member of one of the SOE *reseaux* in Paris when the Resistance was only measured in hundreds, not the tens of thousands who sprang up in 1945. He'd been employed by SNCF, the French State Railway, and his reports on German troop movements and their timetables were invaluable. He was a quiet man and gladly saw it all end, but two or three

54

of his *reseau* kept in touch in the postwar years. They noticed the sellout to Coca-Cola, to IBM, to *le drug-store* and *le pub*. There were other groups who came together when *les pieds noirs* and the rebel generals threatened mutiny in Algiers. And in the time of terror when the OAS was seeking vengeance on the General himself, it seemed natural that the Gaullists should use some of their wartime skills in the service of the President and the Fifth Republic.

ANDERS HAD STAKED OUT the Bricklayer's Arms for two days, lunchtime and nighttime, but there'd been nobody answering Levi's description of the Pole. On the third evening he was reading the evening paper when he heard someone ask for a vodka. There was some leg-pulling from behind the bar, but he still didn't look up. When he looked around the room a few minutes later he saw him. Blue denim trousers, a loose black sweater, and the rest of the description tallied. Nearly six feet, reddish fair hair and a full beard, and a broken nose. He was sitting on his own in the corner watching four men playing darts. Anders moved over to the bar and waited till the landlord was free.

"Landlord."

"Sir. What can I get you?"

Anders laid an ordinary CID warrant card flat on the bar top and said quietly, "Landlord, I'm going into your other bar—the saloon. I want to speak to you there." He slid the warrant back into his hand and nodding at the landlord said, "Good night, then. See you tomorrow, maybe."

The landlord responded, "Righto, sir. Take care."

Anders stood in the street for a moment and then opened the door marked SALOON, saw the landlord nod, and went in.

"Now, officer, what can I do for you?"

"The redheaded man in the corner with a beard, the one who ordered a vodka. What do you know about him?"

The landlord frowned in concentration. "He's been here a few times in the last couple of months. Used to be Friday nights only, or maybe Saturday. Been in more often these last two or three weeks. Some sort of an artist or photographer, I think—something like that, anyway. Doesn't talk much. He's a foreigner, of course. Don't know what; they're all the same to me. Got an accent, though."

"Any idea where he lives?"

"Somewhere off New King's Road near the garage. I may be wrong, but I think that's where."

"Nothing else?"

"No, chief, that's about it."

"Check if he's still there."

The landlord moved behind the bar, turned his head away, and then turned back, wiped a wet glass with a cloth, and nodded.

Anders waited in the darkness on the other side of the street. It was nearly closing time when the man came out. He didn't look up the street toward Anders, just walked down to New King's Road and turned right. Anders went to the corner and watched him. He was walking slowly. He could only be going to Manor Street, a short street of dingy houses. Anders took out his handkerchief and the taxi came out of the darkness but facing the wrong way. "Turn round for the other end of Manor Street, but quick." Two minutes later the taxi stopped, doused its lights, and Anders got out and turned the corner into Manor Street. They were at opposite ends of the street, and Anders could see the man in the streetlights. He was almost up to him when his quarry turned into a derelict garden, went up the short flagged pathway, and disappeared into the darkness of the porch.

Anders was past the house now but he heard the front door slam. The man was inside.

Anders slowed, stopped, and then turned back and walked the half-dozen paces to the shadow of one of the pillars at the garden gate. It was a rusty iron gate hanging on one hinge, permanently propped open. It said number 17. There was no noise from inside the house, and after a few moments Anders walked quietly up the path, paused, and then trod carefully and quietly up the five stone steps. He stood on the mat in the porch and there was a slight reflection from a streetlamp on the frosted glass of the big window in the door. He knew there would be a big round doorknob and a simple lock. Somebody went by in the street whistling out of tune, and Anders waited till all was quiet again. He trod carefully as he moved inside the porch and put his hand gently on the big metal doorknob. He was turning the knob gently when his arm touched a warm body, and as it did, someone standing in the dark beside him said, "OK, open it and go in—don't try to be clever," and to add emphasis the man laid the cold flat barrel of an automatic along Anders' cheek.

When they got to the small landing at the top of a flight of stairs the man reached around Anders, holding the gun in his left hand and turning a key with his right. There was a large room with a modern open staircase to a loft, comfortably furnished with low-level Swedish stuff, and on the walls were large photographs of landscapes and still lifes.

"Put your hands up and on the wall."

The man took everything from Anders' pockets and massaged him expertly for a gun. He sorted through his haul, but there was nothing to identify Anders except a number engraved on the nib of his Parker 52 and he didn't look that carefully.

When the man had finished checking, he said,

"Turn round. That's OK. Now, who are you and why were you following me?"

"I think you've made a mistake. I'm not following you." He was still speaking as the pistol hit his face. As he looked at the man he could feel blood dripping across his left eye, which was swelling and closing, and there was the warm salt taste in his mouth. Instinct told him that if he didn't get this man quickly he probably wouldn't get him at all.

The man moved back to a desk by the window and, still watching Anders, groped around to pull open one of the drawers, and when his hand came out it was holding a long, thin, black cylinder. Anders recognized it immediately—it was a silencer for the Walther pistol the man was holding. Anders had stripped the threads on half a dozen such silencers in the armory, trying to assemble them. He knew that the silencer was far too heavy for the gun, which made it hard to screw the two together even when you were not under pressure. He watched as the man moved the silencer to the barrel of the pistol. He turned it twice but the threads wouldn't take. Anders reckoned the man would have to look down for a split second, and as he watched the fingers turn the silencer he saw it take and start to screw in. He had no doubt why the man was fitting the silencer. He was five feet away but the silencer still wasn't more than half in. As Anders jumped the man hesitated, knowing that it would be dangerous to fire with the silencer loose, and then Anders had both hands around the pistol. The silencer fell away and clattered to the floor. The man's left hand was clawing Anders' face and the gun was pointing down between Anders' feet. He put both hands around the man's wrist and threw himself down. The man came with him, and as he lurched forward Anders' shoulder took him in the belly and he cartwheeled over. The gun hung from a finger and then fell loose, but Anders went for the man himself, who rolled away from him. As the man turned, Anders kicked at the special place behind the hip where the sciatic nerve is most exposed, and the man screamed because the pain was unbearable and his leg was drawn up tight in paralysis. Anders stooped for the Walther and pulled back the slide, and a live round ejected from the chamber. He let the slide spring back and the gun was ready to fire again. He waited for a moment but the man was helpless, his face drained of blood and his right leg trembling and useless.

Anders made a phone call, then sat down and waited. It was nearly half an hour later when he heard them coming up the stairs. Commander Bryant was the first in the room and he looked around, took it all in, and said to one of his men, "Sergeant, you watch this fellow, and you two do a full search of the place." He put his hand on Anders' arm and looking at his face said, "Let's get that cleaned up first." The second door he opened was the bathroom. While he was bathing the swellings and cuts on Anders' face, he asked, "Who is this guy, or do you want to keep it for yourself?"

"He was the man the coins were for. Almost certain to be Z-Eleven or KGB, maybe both. I was tailing him but he was better than me. Must have spotted me back at the pub. He did the old trick—closed the door as if he'd gone inside and then waited for me."

One of the searchers put his head around the door. "There's a lot of stuff here, Commander. Short-wave radio transmitter, one of the new ones, the first I've seen. A full scale darkroom with books of negatives. The usual tin of talcum wth a microdot reader. And these." And he held out the two halves of the false coin.

Anders said quickly, "Was there anything in it— microfilm or anything like that?"

The Special Branch man shook his head. "No, sir, but we'll have a look around."

60

Ten minutes later he was back again.

"It's OK, sir. I think we've got what you want—it was still in the enlarger. He must have forgotten it. It was stuck to the condenser, so we didn't spot it first time." He turned to Commander Bryant. "What do we do with the bod, sir?"

Bryant looked at Anders.

"I'd like him taken to the safe place—the studio," Anders said.

Bryant nodded to his man. "Do that, will you? Hand him over to Daniels in the taxi and go with him."

Anders said, "Can you get the microfilm blown up and sent across to NSA for them to decode? It's urgent."

Bryant nodded. "Won't be necessary. They sent back the code with the first one. I'll pass it to Central Coding—"

Anders interrupted. "Not the film itself, please, just a blowup."

Anders spent an hour on his own in the comfortable rooms. He wanted to get the feel of the man before he interrogated him. It was almost dawn when he hailed a taxi in King's Road. It dropped him in Grosvenor Road on the Embankment, and he walked from there to the studio. The man was in one of the small cells, and Anders looked through the porthole at him. He looked worried. Anders moved through to his flat and then remembered the girl. He knocked on her door, and when she called he went in. The bedside lamp was on and the girl was in bed reading. He sat on the bed and she put down the book. It was a Livres de Poche edition of *Lettres de mon Moulin*. He wondered why that.

"Have you been to—" He had nearly asked if she'd been to England before and he remembered the notes from Mac just in time.

But she was SIS trained and it wouldn't do. She said softly, "It doesn't matter any more. I shall get used to

London." He tried hard to think of a way of apologizing but he was too tired, and while he was thinking, she said, "Have you got medical supplies?"

When he looked surprised she laughed. "For your face—it needs penicillin powder. It's raw, and that's when you pick up infections."

When she'd fixed his face he stood up and said, "Good night."

The girl said, *"Dobranoc,"* and he smiled at her Polish. It hurt his face, but he reckoned they both needed a smile.

9

CENTRAL CODING had the stuff back to Anders by noon the next day. His office in the rambling studio building was revealing of the man, as was the fact that the office and a small bedroom down the corridor were his only home. There was no retreat from this world which was his work and his life.

There was one wall of shelves packed tight with books. A Sony stereo cassette player and a pair of Tandberg speakers. Fishing rods suspended on nails and reaching across one wall. Some photographs: the tennis team at the Defense College, 1962, which included an unsmiling Lieutenant Anders; a press picture of Hitler grinning with hysteria outside Warsaw in 1939; a group of somber-faced officers standing beside an open pit, the grave of the massacred Polish officers at Katyn; a photograph of a man who looked like a perky, aggressive cockerel, named Montgomery; a framed page from the *Saturday Evening Post* that was an advertisement for soap showing the face of a young girl with big eyes, a full soft mouth, and soft, blond, out-of-focus hair; a photo portrait of Vladimir Y. Semichastny, the current, and youngest-ever, head of the KGB. The walls were all plain white and the predominant color of curtains and furnishings was red.

Anders was six feet two, broad-shouldered and solid. Hair almost crew-cut, but black and curly, Slav cheekbones, and a brownness of skin that was not just from sunshine and fitness. The hands were the big strong hands of a rugby player, although Anders never played the game. He considered getting hurt for fun an exclusively English pastime. Russians would take him for a Russian, Poles for a Pole, and the English didn't notice one way or the other.

The two messages on microfilm had given the names of the Frenchmen, a password, their location, and the four stages of the operation as contact, planning, execution, and protest. It named contacts in Canada, the United States, Scandinavia, and Germany. This was going to be too big for Anders to operate on his own, but he decided to interrogate the KGB man before contacting SIS for a re-planning meeting.

Krezki had not slept much. He couldn't make his mind up about what attitude to adopt toward his captors. They were obviously some part of the British Secret Service, but how much did they know? There was nothing much they could get from his room, apart from the radio and a few oddments, which wouldn't prove a thing. He'd got diplomatic immunity as the ambassador's chauffeur. They'd guess he was Z-11, but they couldn't do a thing about the operation; even he had only half the story. He finally decided that he would admit to being Z-11 and then they'd probably ship him out as *persona non grata*.

If it hadn't been that he'd fallen foul of this particular bit of SIS, his reasoning would have been sound enough.

Anders had him brought in at four in the afternoon.
"Name?"
"Krezki, Pawel."
"Born?"

"Lwow, sixth January 1925."

"Occupation?"

"Chauffeur to His Excellency Borowski, the Polish Ambassador to London."

"Are you on the embassy staff?"

"Yes. I have full diplomatic immunity."

Anders looked at him and half smiled. "Well, let's not waste time. What was the transmitter for?"

"I'm a radio ham."

"Registered?"

Krezki wasn't sure, but he reckoned they'd automatically cover him properly. "Yes."

"Call sign?"

Krezki shrugged and gave up. "I'm an officer of the Polish Security Forces, and I have no intention of talking any further."

"You mean you are operating as a spy in this country?"

Krezki didn't answer.

Anders stood up, moved around the desk, and sat on the desk opposite Krezki. Then to Krezki's horror his interrogator spoke in Russian.

"Krezki, we're both in the same business. You're going to tell me the lot. You can do it now and I'll bear your cooperation in mind. Or you can do it the hard way." Anders pointed at the plasters down the left side of his face. "I really don't mind which way we go, they both suit me. One's easy, the other would be a pleasure."

Krezki looked at the gray eyes and the stony face. He'd seen faces like that in Moscow and he knew the reputations that went with them. This man was a killer. Not a killer in hot blood. Not even a rough boy for the enjoyment of some sadistic urge or a sense of power. That kind could have twinges about it afterward. This man was the kind who didn't kill with lust, or have regrets when it was over; they killed because it was necessary and part of a pattern, like switching off a light. They didn't seek an excuse; it was part of a chess game. If their opponent made a certain move, they countered automatically and formally. The victim decided, not them. Anders didn't move while Krezki looked up at him.

"What happens if I cooperate?"

"Depends on how far you cooperate and the nature of your operation. What do you want to happen?"

Krezki sighed deeply, then looked up again. "Stay here, I suppose."

Anders nodded. "We'll see." He walked back around to his seat and leaned forward, elbows on the desk. "Tell me about the Frenchmen." And Krezki started talking.

Marie-Claire Foubert booked in at the Hilton. She asked for the fifteenth floor and got room 1501. There was just a little light left, and as she looked out of the window she could see the model cars crawling down Park Lane and across the road to Apsley House, the home of Napoleon's old enemy. Farther on still was an arch in a square of lawn that looked like the Arc de Triomphe. In the next hour she moved around the hotel checking the restaurants and bars, the shops, the service areas, and the exits, and finally she bought a pack of Gauloises, that morning's *Figaro*, and the French edition of *Vogue*. She'd checked the three rooms on the fifth floor occupied by the Frenchmen, and now it was just a question of time. They'd been waiting for nearly two weeks, so they were probably getting bored or impatient.

For over an hour she sat in the corner of the main bar, reading her papers and sipping a well-made martini. During that time she was propositioned crudely by Arabs, with enthusiasm by Swedes, with boyish charm by Americans, and was merely looked at with lust by Englishmen. She had just ordered her third drink when one of

66

the Frenchmen came in: tall, slim, pale-faced, American suit, bow tie, hands on hips, and an air of being very pleased with himself. He looked at the girl and then looked away, snapped his fingers to a waiter, and ordered a drink. She guessed he was Corsican or from the Italian border area; he had the massive vulgarity of Italian men without the charm that went with it. The snapping of fingers was for her benefit, and while he stood waiting for the drink he looked her over and finally walked over to her table. "Anyone sitting here?"

She shook her head and went on reading. When his drink came he gave an extravagant tip. His eyes took in her sweater and the long shapely legs.

The pickup lacked grace, and she made clear she was bored throughout the meal he invited her to. Afterward he took her to the 007 bar. She refused to dance and left him by ten o'clock but promised to have tea with him the next day. His name, he said, was André Prouvost.

10

THE MEETING WAS IN ONE of the SIS houses in Queen
Anne's Gate. At the big round table was the Director of
Operations SIS, Sir John Walker; Major Anders; the
Foreign Office liaison officer to SIS, James Kent; and a
liaison officer from CIA, Jake Salis. There were no pa-
pers on the table, and Sir John opened the talk.

"Well, you've all been briefed on the state of the
game, and as Major Anders suggested that this was now
more than a one-man operation I feel it would be better
if we included you gentlemen in our thinking at this
stage. I'd better explain our various roles. Major Anders
will still be in control of the operation. James Kent from
the Foreign Office is here because there may be diplomatic moves to be made at a high level and he can help
us there. Jake Salis is seconded to us from CIA and is
also acting for the Special Branch of the Royal Canadian
Mounted Police—CIA and NSA facilities are available
and it can be assumed that Canada and the USA are as
interested in defusing this little lot as we are. Now,
Major Anders, bring us all up to date."

"We know that this is a KGB operation using the
Polish Intelligence setup Z-Eleven and a group of Frenchmen. It's organized like a typical KGB operation. It's
overcomplex, and we are picking up the pieces fast. We
have both parts of the instructions, but they only cover
general intentions and contact. The rest of the operation

was to come through the Pole, Krezki. I've got him. He's talked, but there's more information due from Moscow. The Frenchmen, or the active group anyway, are at the Hilton and they have been contacted by the girl. NSA people have broken the KGB code. I've got radio transmission times from Moscow and the network time and wavelength the Pole was using for his traffic. The radio hasn't been used much yet, communication has been mainly by microfilm, but they're bound to use radio as things get moving. There are—"

Sir John interrupted and looked at the CIA man. "Jake, you wanted to ask something?"

"Yes, sir, I'd like to ask Major Anders how cooperative Krezki will be. Could we turn him completely, including the radio?"

Anders looked at Sir John and got a nod of approval. "So far he's cooperated. If I hurry him into the radio, I feel he may dig his heels in. He's waiting now to see what sort of deal we'll give him."

Jake Salis looked across to Anders. "Any idea what he wants?"

"A pension—I'd say he'd settle for fifteen hundred to two thousand pounds a year. Initial protection. He probably wants to end up in Australia." Anders smiled. "Somewhere a long way from here, anyway."

Sir John leaned back. "Sounds easy enough, Tad. What's he up to at the moment?"

"I've left him to rot for a couple of days. I want him to feel we've no great need for him now; he was getting a bit cocky. I think I could get him to play along with us if I talked about a cash bonus and a bit of the fleshpots of London." He stopped and looked around the table.

James Kent of the Foreign Office spoke up. "I'm going to prepare some answers for the press. Point out the difficulty—impossibility—of anybody launching an invasion to liberate Europe across three thousand miles of the Atlantic. And without giving any details at all, I've given instructions to our people in the countries concerned to keep their ears open for chitchat in any area that touches on attitudes to the United States."

Sir John nodded in agreement. "Now, what sort of help do you want, Tad?"

"Well, sir, right now I want access to an explosives man. I'm not at all up to date. But the main thing is that I've got a feeling that this is a much bigger operation than we've uncovered so far. They're taking it very slowly, really, and there's no sign that they are ready. I think they're waiting for something to happen before they get to the next stage. This operation would be the most valuable coup for the Soviets since the U-2, and a much bigger payoff. I think that the French have had the basic idea and they probably contacted the Poles for finance, and the Poles sold the idea to the KGB, who've seen its possibilities and are going to make it much bigger than the Frenchmen expected. I'd like a full support operation to back me up—evaluating what I get, checking on all newcomers to Communist embassies and missions, full radio monitoring, and checks on Soviet sleepers in the UK. I'll look after the penetration and control, but it needs more than that to make sure I'm well briefed on any indications from other sources."

Before Sir John could reply, James Kent said, "Major, is there any reason why you can't deal with these Frenchmen straight away?"

"Well, right now we at least know where the action is. If I wipe this lot out they won't abandon the operation. Let's face it, we were lucky to uncover this at all. If they start afresh we may never contact the next lot and the first we'll know will be from newspaper headlines and then the explosions to whip up more bad blood."

James Kent frowned. "Why explosions? That's the first I've heard—"

"The contact in the KGB house in Paris is a sabo-

70

tage and explosives expert. That's not an accident. The newspaper leak would create tensions, but staged protests—demonstrations, explosions, and so on—would mean a real escalation, and what's more it could keep it all at boiling point for months. A bit like the Arabs and Israel." Then Anders looked across at Sir John. "Sir, I must get back to my place. Can I leave what I've asked for to you—and the others?"

"Right. I'll keep in touch through the studio."

The girl had been waiting in Anders' office for nearly half an hour and she'd wandered around looking at the clues to this strange man. He was a loner, that was for sure. No country's secret service allowed emotional attachments between its operators, but sex was another thing. But this man was odd, aware of her and concerned for her safety and her feelings but nothing more. Like most men, when he was talking to her he looked at her face as if he enjoyed it, but unlike other men his eyes didn't wander to her sweater. Maybe he was a queer. He was easy to talk to, charming—yet somehow not involved. But from what little Mac had told her there had been girls. And among the books was a Palgrave, and marking a page among the Shakespeare sonnets was a slip of paper with some lines of verse, and she recognized Anders' writing. She'd read it several times.

Like truthless dreams, so are my joys expired,
Beyond recall are all my dappled days.

And in what was either a Polish or Russian Bible there was a small, creased, and faded photograph of a stone cottage with a young woman and a small boy standing at the gate. The woman's hand was resting on the small boy's shoulder, and the boy was looking up at the woman's smiling face. The small boy could have been Anders.

The room was quiet and still, like a dog waiting

patiently for its master. She felt secure, and her peace was somehow not destroyed even when Anders came in, said "Hello," and bounced his briefcase onto the desk and sat down.

He looked across at her and sat still with his arms on the arms of his chair. "You look different—still beautiful, but different."

She smiled and said nothing.

Then he grinned. "You've changed your hair and that's a new white sweater."

She nodded. "Lover boy bought me the sweater." Then, as if to cut the conversation about herself, she went on. "I've been having meals with all of them yesterday and today. They had a phone call from Stockholm this morning. They seem very tense since then. I got the impression they're expecting someone—someone important. And they're going to rent a house. They've had lists from estate agents, mainly in the Thames valley. I'm going with lover boy tomorrow morning to look at one."

"Where?"

"I don't know, but we're going to have lunch at a pub called the Bull at Bisham." Anders wrote the name down. When he'd finished, the girl said, "They've got valuables in the hotel safe. I don't know what they are, but I saw a receipt for five packages."

The general manager of the London Hilton was not fond of policemen or intelligence men—they always meant trouble. He reckoned there must be something about the London Hilton that attracted IRA men, Arab terrorists, and Dutch arms dealers. Why the hell didn't they give the Inn on the Park a turn? He sighed as he passed the SIS identity card back to Anders. "What is it you want, Mr. Anders?"

"I'd like to look at packages deposited in your safe

by guests in these rooms." He pushed a paper across the desk. The manager put half an eye to it, but he wasn't so concerned with "who" as "what."

"Do the packages contain arms or explosives?"

"Unlikely."

"Stolen goods?"

"Not in the sense you mean."

The manager shook his head. "I'm sorry, I can't help you, Mr. Anders. A guest at the Hilton is entitled to expect that what he leaves in our safe will be treated with security and confidentiality. Except for arms and stolen goods, I don't even have discretion to allow you to have access to items deposited by guests." He waved his hand dismissively when he saw Anders was about to speak. "It's all right, Mr. Anders. You have indicated that your people consider this of great importance, and our organization cooperates where appropriate with all governments where we have hotels. I will give you a New York number, and if one of your officials will contact that number they can give me clearance. Better than that I cannot do."

"May I use your telephone?"

"By all means, by all means. Would you like me to leave?"

Anders shook his head and phoned Special Branch. Seven minutes later the clearance came from New York. The general manager smiled.

"Well, Mr. Anders, I've never known the GPO and the Bell Telephone Company to be quite that efficient before. If you will excuse me I shall ask our chief security officer to assist you. Good-bye."

The hotel security man was an ex-inspector from D Division, and when the packages had been removed from the safe he said, "D'you want a kettle, Mr. Anders?"

Anders laughed. "No, thanks, that was good enough in the old days, but if you steam open with a knife you can see the marks of the blade afterwards."

He took a small aerosol from his case and lightly sprayed the flaps of the envelopes. He opened the thick packages first. There were almost $20,000 in American Express traveler's checks, $30,000 in cash, together with £25,000 in Bank of England notes. There were Irish, British, and Swedish passports for each of the Frenchmen. The large flat envelope was the last. There were a number of photographed documents. A letter from President Roosevelt to Churchill, a similar letter from Mackenzie King, an original document from the Nazis' Forschungs Amt—this was a decoded signal from Roosevelt to the United States Ambassadors to Vichy and Moscow—and finally a brief report from Donald Maclean in Moscow suggesting how to approach the British press, with a note on how the D notice system worked.

Anders photographed the documents and every page of the passports and returned them to the envelopes. Before he put back the passports he laid a thin metal rod across the photographs. It made no mark on them but there would be a wide mauve band when the passports were examined under the special light at any alien's checkout point.

Anders bought an *Evening Standard* at the Hilton kiosk, and as he was turning toward the foyer he saw the girl. She was with the Frenchman, and as they came out of the lift the man put his arm around her waist as if he owned her and for a moment Anders felt a flash of jealousy. They moved toward a phone booth and Anders hesitated, then slowly walked down the stairs, past the fountain and the flower shop, and out the back entrance. As he walked past the flower shop windows there was a tall vase in the center with superb red roses. The full orange-scarlet heads on long graceful stems made him think of the girl. He was still thinking of her and the roses when he got to the corner of Hertford Street. He stood and watched the flashy cars and their owners pulling up at the gambling casino. Like most people in his business Anders observed the rest of humanity without indulging in value judgments, but on odd occasions when he was overtired or disorganized he made comparisons, and this was one of those times. It was Saturday evening and the world was going about its business of enjoying itself, and he wondered if they would be shocked or disbelieving if they knew what went on to preserve their freedom, and he wondered if some of the freedoms were worth preserving. But behind it all he was thinking of the girl. It seemed an arid, wasted life for a woman, and on an impulse he turned back, went through the swing doors, and bought the roses. They were full and fragrant; the neat little label said *One dozen Soraya.* Back at the studio in Pimlico he put them on her bed.

He used the scrambler phone to the house in Hampshire and then brought in Krezki.

He went through the motions of making a deal with Krezki, who asked for $3,000 to monitor Moscow and to make one transmission. He brought over one of the coding specialists and a security radio operator to code the transmission material and to supervise Krezki. There were no problems, and Moscow got the news that Krezki had left the embassy because of security problems, had good cover, and awaited further instructions. The last two words of the message were checks to show he'd got both sets of microfilm instructions.

When Anders was alone again he put on a cassette. It was Jacqueline du Pré playing the Elgar cello concerto, and he leaned back with his arms behind his head, too tired to move to the comfortable chairs. The music was typical of all that was good of these people, the English. It was why he loved them. But he knew that when the genes of his English mother and his Polish father had intermingled to program his character and temperament, all the genes of motive had been his father's. He was English, but another self—a Pole—stood outside and watched him. The Pole did, the Englishman thought—always separate, never together. They were not a happy mixture, and he knew it. They needed a catalyst to fuse them more easily. About halfway through the third movement the door opened and the girl was standing there. She stood looking at him and then slid into one of his armchairs and putting her head back listened to the music. When it ended she looked across at him, and he saw she had tears in her eyes.

"Did you like the music?"

She nodded. "Yes, but I liked the roses more. Why did you do that?"

He shrugged. "I'd just seen you, I saw the flowers, they made me think of you, so I bought them—simple as that."

The girl was silent for a time. Then she stood up. When she opened the door she turned. "They've bought a car. A Jag, secondhand. It's being delivered tomorrow morning to the hotel. They put off the house visit till tomorrow. They wanted to wait till they'd got the car."

"What's the registration number of the car?"

"GBH four-nine-one G—it's white." She stood looking at him for a moment, then closed the door behind her.

Anders phoned the technical radio section and gave them brief instructions and the car number. Just after midnight they had traced the car to a showroom in Piccadilly, and when they left there it was just getting light. Six troopers of the Household Cavalry were turning their horses into St. James, ignoring the one-way signs; they were admired by two cleaning ladies and cursed by a taxi driver.

Anders was shaving, and although he didn't realize it he was humming the melody of a little ditty by Jacques Brel called "Litanie pour un amour." Another day had started.

11

THE WHITE JAG turned where the sign said TEMPLE
¾ MILE and, following the winding muddy lane to the
big gates, turned down the drive marked THE MILL
HOUSE. The girl went in with the Frenchman and they
looked over the house. It had once been a mill, taking
its power from the rushing Thames waters that slid over
Temple weir. The house was big and rambling and the
furniture was old but not valuable. From the garden of
the house a wooden bridge on piles jutted out over the
water to join the catwalk over the weir that led to the
small island where the lockkeeper's cottage was set between two big elms. The Frenchman carefully checked
the stables and outhouses.

They had lunch at the Bull at Bisham, and between
courses the man went over a large-scale map of Temple
and Marlow. After lunch he drove the Jag up the M4
to the Chiswick overpass and back, timing the journey
both ways. He told the girl to stay in the car as he
made a phone call from the call box outside the Marlow
post office. Ten minutes later, in the estate agent's office,
the Frenchman had read through the lease, signed it, and
paid the first quarter's rent in cash. They took the keys
and drove back to the house. The light was beginning
to go, and they watched the boats lining up on the far
side of the river to go through the lock before it closed
for the night.

He timed the journey back to the overpass at twenty-four minutes without exceeding the speed limit, and it took thirty-four minutes to cover the last few miles to the Hilton. Later that night the girl phoned Anders and gave him the details of the house and the news that she and the Frenchman were going down the next day to stock up. The others would be going down when the man who had phoned arrived from Stockholm.

There's a shop with a small window and a narrow entrance halfway down the Kungsgatan in Stockholm. Men of all shapes and sizes go through the narrow entrance, and very few glance at the girlie magazines displayed in the small window. The real stuff's inside. Whether you want your porn in black and white, full-color litho, on film, or on gramophone records, and in any one of five languages, this is Stockholm's place for connoisseurs. There are no pictures of old slags and tattooed sailors here. The girls in the pictures are young and pretty and even the Great Danes are registered at the Swedish Kennel Club.

The man had a leathery, weathered face and from his good tweed jacket to his tan suede boots he stuck out a mile as an Englishman, although because of the crew cut of his gray hair he could have been an American. He turned the pages of one of the magazines, put it down, and grinning at the proprietor said, "Vous avez que'que chose de bon en français?"

The proprietor looked at him, surprised; then, recovering, he shrugged. "Ça dépend, m'sieu—vous avez besoin de quelque chose?"

The big man laughed. "Ah, oui, une jeune blonde avec les jambes jusqu'au derrière."

This was the man all right but nothing like what the proprietor had expected. The small shop owed nearly half its turnover to the KGB. It not only provided perfect cover with its stream of male customers, but its cash trade in many currencies made the movement of money easy and undetectable. But KGB men were always so drab. He'd never had one like this before, but the passwords were all in order and he had been told that this one was something special. He pulled out a key ring and used a key in each of the two locks on the door at the back of the shop. He opened the door halfway and followed the Russian inside. There were half a dozen comfortable chairs and a film projector on a small table facing a large white screen. And there was a pretty young blonde, typically Swedish, and she was wearing only a tiny pair of briefs. The Russian clicked his heels and, half smiling, gave a little bow to the girl.

"I see you have film shows, Mr. Erlander."

The proprietor turned to the girl. "You can go now, Kirstin. No need to come back till tomorrow."

The Russian held up a massive paw. "Certainly not, Mr. Erlander." He was looking appreciatively at the girl. "Our business won't take many minutes, and I'd be glad of some company for tonight." He changed to Russian and was a bit sharper, less charming. "You've got the package and the pictures, I suppose."

The proprietor nodded and answered in Russian. "Yes, comrade. Do you want them now?"

"Best get it done."

The Swede went behind a curtain in the corner of the room and came back with a thick brown envelope which he held out to the big man, who said, "Everything's there?"

"Everything, comrade."

"I'm leaving for Bromma at eight in the morning. I'll stay here for the night, yes?"

"Of course, whatever you wish."

With that the big Russian changed back to Swedish and walking over to the girl said, "And what's your name?"

"Kirstin Swenholm."

The Russian was smiling and looking down at her

two full breasts and their rosy pink nipples. "And are you going to look after me this evening, Kirstin?"

The girl darted a quick glance at the Swede, who nodded, and barely had time to say "yes" before the big strong hands were closing over her breasts. As the proprietor closed the door behind him, he heard the girl laugh at something the Russian had said.

This was the first full colonel of the KGB that had come his way. They'd said he was special and he certainly was. Looked like a well-off American, built like a professional football player, so sure of himself that he didn't check the package—and it had cost the KGB $10,000 plus expenses. Amiable and easygoing and playing around with the girl before he'd even left the room. Even the regulars didn't do that.

But the girl wasn't surprised. She stood patiently while he fondled her, and she laughed when he told her to take off the briefs. She was not embarrassed when he sat down at the table and watched her step out of them or when he looked at her when she stood naked in front of him. The surprise came when he told her to sit down and reached for the package on the table. She noticed that there were several blue wax seals which he broke carefully and then put the bits in his pocket. He pulled out the contents and spread them on the table. A lot of glossy photographs and six or seven folded sheets of paper. The man spread them out one by one. They looked like architects' plans—there were red lines and circles marked on them—and when he looked through the photographs they weren't the kind of photographs she was used to. They were of rooms with high ceilings and corridors and stairways. There must have been over a hundred.

The big man looked pleased. When he had put them all back in the big envelope, and the envelope in his jacket pocket, things got back to normal and her ego was restored. He looked at her, his eyes enjoying her body, and reached out and pulled her over till she was standing in front of him. And the things he did and the things he said were the things she was used to. Mr. Erlander changed the 200 rubles for her next day.

The big Russian collected his two bags from left luggage at Bromma airport and caught a scheduled flight to Prestwick. Never going for number two, Igor Rudenko, colonel in the KGB, hired a Hertz car and drove to Newcastle, where, as the Swedish architect Sven Eklund, he took a normal North East Airlines flight to London. He booked in at the Europa in Grosvenor Square, and when he was settled in his room he phoned the London Hilton.

The Red Army Ensemble was at the Albert Hall that evening, and he gave them his support. He made a note to report to Madam Furtsewa at the Ministry of Culture about their ridiculous rendering of "It's a Long Way to Tipperary." The bloody oafs stood there as if they were on guard outside the Lubyanka, singing like drunken Cossacks at the top of their voices, obviously not aware that you don't belt out an Irish love song like a Red Army marching song. No wonder the English tittered. Never mind, the poor bastards would be back in Moscow by the weekend and he'd probably got at least another three months of the fleshpots of London. A friend had once told him that he'd read in Rudenko's personal file that "the subject is a womanizer and fond of Western life." He'd laughed; he didn't give a damn. When there was a real tough operation in the West he always got it. They needed something better than the usual Volga boatmen from time to time, and he was the only one they had.

Department C-11 of the CID monitored the call to the Hilton, and the tape went to Anders ten minutes after they'd taken a copy.

12

WHEN THE WHITE JAG was doing more than 50 mph it was difficult for Security Signals to monitor conversations, but the bleeper transmitter they'd fixed behind the radiator grille gave them a strong permanent signal —enough to plot its movements. The Frenchmen had obviously chosen the house because it was not only isolated but gave quick, easy access to London via the M4, and it probably wasn't a coincidence that London Airport was only about fifteen minutes from either end.

Every room in the house and outbuildings had been photographed, and the upper floor of the lockkeeper's cottage had been taken over as a monitoring center. A video camera with a 1,000-mm lens covered the garden and most of the main access to the house.

Spreading down westward from the house along the Berkshire bank of the Thames was a line of pontoon moorings. Nearly a quarter of a mile from the house, on mooring number five, was a 40-foot Bates Starcraft which Anders had hired from the boatyard. The MV *Donna Tomara* was well out of sight of the house, and its slightly longer aerials would not be noticed in the flurry of radar equipment sprouting from most of the other big boats alongside.

Anders sat patiently in the boat waiting for the last light to go. A stiff breeze had set off a crosscurrent on the surface of the river, and the big boat swung at her moorings. The cries of the moorhens gradually ceased and there was quiet except for the distant hum of traffic on the new bypass. There were lights in the lockkeeper's cottage, and when Anders switched on the small VHF radio he cut into the traffic between a Pan Am 747 and ground control at the airport. He looked up through the hatch at the sky and could see the lights of a 747 as it swung from Marlow back on the entry path to Heathrow.

When Anders got to a big cedar he counted the paces to the high wall that surrounded the house and then the distance to the big double gates. The Frenchman and the girl had left three hours before. The man was at the Hilton and the girl was at the studio in Pimlico.

Anders checked the keys to the three outside doors and went in through the big front door. There was a vast hall with stone floors and four white palladian columns and a wide staircase that led to the upper house. On each side of the hall were several large rooms with the kind of furnishings that come from country auctions. A big kitchen with an Aga stove that was fueled but not lit. Upstairs there was a landing with oak cupboards and six large furnished bedrooms and two bathrooms. It was much as the estate agent's description. The garden gave onto a cutting to the river. There was a clinker-built dinghy moored to the bank, and in one corner he could just make out the handrail to the wooden structure that led across the rushing waters of the weir. He looked across to the lockkeeper's cottage but could see no sign of the watchers.

Back at the boat he made some notes on the big-scale map, and twenty minutes later he was driving back up the M4 to London.

He decided there was no reason to keep Levi. There was nothing more he wanted from him.

The girl had waited for nearly two hours before she

went back to the Hilton. The phone was ringing as she let herself in to room 1501. It was the Frenchman inviting her to dinner; would she come at eight thirty, not earlier.

There seemed to be great tension in the group of Frenchmen now that the man from Stockholm had arrived. The two older ones, Firette and Loussier, were meeting him today and André Prouvost seemed to think that she would not be able to join them again for meals and drinks. They had much business to discuss now, he explained, but he said that he hoped to get out from the meetings to see her from time to time.

At eight forty-five she pressed the doorbell to the suite and André opened the door. The other two rose when she came in, but the big man was already standing, a full glass to his lips. He turned his head casually to look at her and as he looked she saw all the coldness, the danger, and the power of the man. Then the gray eyes sparkled and the big face creased. "Well, well, André, please introduce me to your friend." And as he held her hand she was conscious of his appeal. He was almost another Tad.

It seemed he was over to discuss Swedish building methods with one of the ministries. "And what brings you here, my dear?" She'd given her cover story and he'd half smiled all the time she was talking. He could merely have been a man who never believed a woman; it was hard to tell. It wasn't quite an interrogation, or it wouldn't have been if she hadn't known what he was. They'd discussed Servan-Schreiber's *Le Défi Américain* and then he'd stood up, said his good-byes, and left.

13

ANDERS THOUGHT SIR JOHN must be thinking about something else while he was talking, but Sir John batted back the ball in due course. "Have you any views as to when they are going to start the operation?"

"Fairly soon, I would think. Taking the house, and then Rudenko arriving, is some indication. But they still don't seem in a hurry."

"What about Krezki?"

"Nothing back from Moscow so far."

"What about the contact at the house in Paris?"

"He's been telephoned every two days, but he's obviously waiting on Moscow."

"Well, I didn't want to put this forward if you had anything else in mind, but I think they're nearly ready to go." He pulled a file from a drawer in his desk and slid it across to Anders. "Read that little lot. Let me know what you think when I get back."

The file held nothing but press clippings. There were nearly fifty, all dated within the last ten days. They covered all the national newspapers, some specialist journals, and most of the important provincials.

The Sunday *Times* color magazine had carried a three-page feature on Joseph Kennedy, the United States Ambassador in London in 1939 and 1940. The piece laid emphasis on his defeatism and forecasts that Hitler would be in London by August 15 and that the United

States should abandon Britain to her fate. His constant advice to Washington not to waste resources by assisting the British was covered, along with his resignation and rapid return to America after London completed its first month under Luftwaffe attack. In case it could be thought that old Joe Kennedy was the odd Kennedy out, there was a picture of him and his son, John Kennedy, at the start of their journey from London to attend the coronation of the Pope.

The same weekend the *Observer* had carried a long and well-researched article which pointed out the huge American influence in British industry and emphasized the fact that the United States' stake was growing twice as fast as the rest of the UK economy. It showed that in some industries American-financed companies controlled 80 percent of the UK market.

There was a whole page in a computer journal bitterly attacking the trading policies of IBM, including a warning about software and spare parts in time of war, with a warning that it couldn't be taken for granted that in wartime the UK and the USA would have common interests. A similar but shorter piece in a financial weekly advised the prudent company to buy ICL computers. There was a series of articles on the baleful influence on the British economy of the American car manufacturers in Britain, with a recommendation to buy British—"And we mean British owned, not just British made."

There were milder pieces, but with more feminine acid, covering the wide difference between the selling price and the actual cost of materials used in American cosmetics, in several women's magazines. Over half the nationals' women's pages carried the same basic story. There was a medical report in two women's magazines implying the exploitation of children as a market by manufacturers of dangerous American bottled and canned drinks. A science journal detailed the number of

British inventions and discoveries from penicillin to the jet engine which had been exploited by the Americans, with the British left out in the cold. Even family magazines carried pieces casting doubts on the nutritional value of well-known breakfast cereals and "so-called improved" baby foods.

There were five separate items on Canadian subjects, ranging from the overcautious use of Canadian troops in World War II, to the detriment of British servicemen, to a careful analysis which showed that there were close economic and military links between the USA and Canada which did not extend to London. They were all well written and in many cases supported by official statistics. Most of them carried no by-line apart from "A special correspondent." There was almost nothing untrue in any item; it was more a matter of emphasis rather than distortion, and if the campaign had been in the hands of a PR consultancy they would have deserved a fat fee and picked up a dozen big accounts when it was written up in *Campaign*.

There wasn't much that hadn't been said before during the previous fifteen years, but for all this material to have been published in a period of ten days meant it was either a campaign or a remarkable coincidence. And as the chief instructor at the Intelligence Training Center always said, "In intelligence work there ain't no such thing as a coincidence."

When Sir John came back he raised his eyebrows at Anders. "Well, what d'you think?"

"Any idea of the sources?"

"Yes, most of the items that can be traced have a Paris origin—they have different contributors but the source is an outfit called Agence Presse Lorraine. It was formed three months ago and its address is the same as Prouvost's *Les Maquisards*. It looks pretty much like the French are going to handle the press side and the Russians will provide the bangs."

At the last count there were 158 KGB operators and 27 members of the GRU—the Russian Army's separate intelligence organization—working in Great Britain. Of their many contacts, casual or otherwise, who covered every aspect of British life—assembled together they would have filled Wembley Stadium—at least a third would have been horrified if they had known that they featured on the card files of the KGB. Some fifty were "sleepers"—committed Communists instructed to penetrate some department or organization and then await instructions that might take years to come.

There was, for example, one Sean O'Malley, age thirty, who lived at number 27A Victoria Road, Aston, Birmingham, some distance down the road from what is called Spaghetti Junction. At the turn of the century Victoria Road had contained the homes of successful artisans, bricklayers, carpenters, patternmakers and iron-foundry foremen. Since then it had gone down in the world and was still sliding, each year, a little nearer to being condemned as unfit for human beings to live in. As late as the 1960s there had been houses without electricity, and only two out of six hundred had a bath-room. Until the war people had been happy enough with gaslight and no baths, but after that the spirit had gone out of the place. In the minds of some, the landlords and the Tory Council were to blame.

Sean O'Malley spent his days on an assembly line at one of the sprawling plants nearby that supplied car bodies for the big Midlands car manufacturers. There were over 6,000 people employed at the plant, on the huge presses, in the paint shop, and on all the rest of the complex process of bashing steel into sports cars and family sedans. Three generations of O'Malleys had lived at 27A, and the rent that had once been two shillings a week was now seven pounds. Sean O'Malley belonged to no political party and he never cast a vote. He was a regular attender at union meetings but had twice refused to be a shop steward; nevertheless, he had more influence on number-two assembly line than anyone else. He was crafty rather than intelligent, a loner by temperament, and he approved of his wife's having a job. He took home about £32 a week average. Once a week he reported on the mood of the shop floor to a man who ran a second-hand bookshop near the old Repertory Theatre, and several times a year they both got instructions from the Soviet Embassy in Kensington. Although he didn't know it, there were thirty-four like-minded souls in the Birmingham–Coventry area who followed much the same pattern.

Some miles to the northwest, currently attending the Labour Party conference in Blackpool, there was the party organizer known simply as Uncle Arthur. Despite the unseasonably good weather, the conference's final session was packed. It was Labour's sixth year in opposition, and as the leader of the party was saying in his winding-up address, "There is a time for discussion, a time for honest differences to be sincerely expressed, but at the end of the day brother must clasp hand with brother and the good of the party in the House of Commons and at the grass roots . . ." etc., etc. Two members of the *Tribune* group exchanged meaningful glances; they'd won their bets—they'd been sold out again. They'd been promised a swingeing attack on the MPs who had voted for the adoption of the latest decree from Brussels. A right-of-center Trades Union delegate and a Midlands MP passed notes because the promised policy statement that the Parliamentary Labour Party was not bound by conference decisions had not even got a mention. The Leader had, after all, threaded his way through the many minefields and, as so often before, had left the delegates holding a winding-up speech that was a sticky bag of licorice.

Uncle Arthur sat comfortably, cigarette ash frosting

90

his expansive waistcoat. He smiled to himself as he looked at the party leaders flanking the speaker: bright boys from university who'd never done a day's real work in their lives and working-class boys who'd shoved their way up through one union and another, forever making meaningless gestures to impress the voters. Bloody fools, the lot of them. None of them really voted for the Labour Party—half of them voted for the *New Statesman* and the other half voted for the *Daily Mirror*. The money, the time, that this bunch had wasted—it made him sick. Uncle Arthur looked benign enough, but when there was a tough battle in a constituency it was his powers of organization and administration they called on. It was reckoned that Uncle Arthur as organizer meant a full turnout and an extra 10 percent on the party's figures. A Tory lady from one of the Surrey constituencies, a leading dispenser of coffee mornings for her party, a busybody for every charity and wife of the constituency chairman, had once lost control because of Uncle's demand for a recount and, flushed with anger, had spat in his face. Uncle Arthur had turned his cheek to a press photographer and said quietly, "Light it from the side, boy, or they'll never see it." It had been right across the front page of all the tabloids next day. He loved it and had used it at two by-elections in the North-East the following month. Uncle Arthur had more contacts and more influence with working men all over the country than any ten Labour politicians you could name. He made about £2,500 a year and expenses for his various services to the party, and about twice as much from the KGB.

Not all the services enjoyed by the KGB required that money change hands. A case in point was Philip Fayne-Waring, en route at the moment to the TV Center in London. The radio in his minicar was on full blast, and he thought he'd arranged things very well, really. By the time he got to Shepherd's Bush he'd have listened to a cycle of Schubert lieder by Fischer-Dieskau. And *Any Questions* on Radio 4 was a must—he was to be on the panel for the first time next week, one of the two "nonpoliticals." And depending on his timing he'd hear the overture and probably all of Act I of *The Bartered Bride* performed by the Czech State Opera Company. The Polish Embassy had given him the same recording after his recorded talk for Radio Moscow on "Charles Dickens and His Times," which was rather nice in a way because he gathered the Poles didn't entirely approve of the Czechs.

When he arrived at the TV Center it was flattering to be recognized by the man at the gate—"Ah—evening, Professor, just go over to your usual place, will you?"— and the white pole had swung up and he had parked the car with a bit of a flourish. Usual place, eh? Not bad, really. Although at thirty-seven he *was* the youngest Regius Professor of History, and the only one who spoke fluent Russian. One of the tabloids had run a large picture of him captioned "New Panel Show Personality." Clearly his wildly enthusiastic and rather spluttering delivery, combined with fair, wavy hair that tended to hang over his eyes sheepdog fashion, was making him something of a TV star.

Tonight's panel discussion was entitled "If the British Empire Was the Answer, What Was the Question?" and oddly enough he'd received last week a most interesting analysis of how the last of the Empire countries like Australia, New Zealand, and Canada had improved their economic and political ties with the United States at the expense of Great Britain. There were a number of very quotable quotes that he hoped to inject. He had noticed too that the Poles had only used United Nations figures, so he could claim complete impartiality.

His sudden rise to TV fame and fan letters had

pleased him no end. He was modest enough to wonder why it had all happened so quickly. It almost seemed that the little cocktail party with the Polish Ambassador at Weymouth Street had brought him luck.

There was a young girl named Tamara Resniak in the research team for *Let's Talk It Over* who could have given him the answer, but nobody asked her.

14

THE MESSAGE FINALLY CAME THROUGH from Moscow for Krezki to contact a Mr. Sven Eklund at the Europa. There had been no answer from the Kléber telephone number for a week. The message had obviously got through about Kujawski's defection. Operation Snowball was now live and under control of the KGB. Krezki passed the word to Eklund at the Europa and Firette at the Hilton.

Some sheep are bred for wool, others for meat, and it's been said that Romney Marsh sheep are bred only for survival. In winter the snow and wind gust across the flat landscape, and for miles the snow blankets the land and nothing seems to move under the gray skies. Even the birds are quiet. But spring comes early and the summers are long and the marshes stand encased in dry, reticulated mud.

That part of Romney Marshes called the Isle of Oxney was still under the sea less than a hundred years ago, and the land that's now exposed is harsh and unkempt. Mole drains and culverts fill from every rainstorm that shrouds the hills to the north. It carries two smallish farms and a small-holding.

The only building on the small-holding, apart from a wooden slatted cottage, is the remains of a kiln. The heavy lorry's engine labored, and its wheels spun in the thick mud of the track to the kiln. They had left the white Jag back at the cottage.

It took two hours to check the contents of the boxes and load them on the three-tonner, and when they were finished the Frenchmen went back to the cottage and paid the small-holder what had been promised.

The lorry, followed by the white Jag, turned onto the Tenterden road and just after midnight they slid down the hill at Goudhurst. They turned west at Sevenoaks and were on the M4 when the false dawn broke.

The boxes were taken inside the house at Temple to a room with barred windows and a new lock on the door. The lorry went back to the hire company at High Wycombe.

The girl was sitting in his office when Anders got back, and she smiled to herself as he went around his desk and sat in the office chair rather than the easy chair next to her. He was pale and drawn, and she hoped her news would please him.

He looked across at her and smiled. "You look as if you've got news for me."

She nodded. "I have. Shall I start?"

He switched on the tape recorder and nodded.

"The Frenchmen have documents that they intend selling or giving—they haven't decided yet—to the newspapers and radio and TV. You probably know all this—the documents are very high level and will show that the Americans and Canadians were ready to make a deal with Hitler." She paused but he didn't speak so she went on. "The Swede at the Europa is Russian, a colonel in the KGB. He's controlling the operation and he's using people from the Polish Z-Eleven."

"Why do the Frenchmen need a Russian to control it?"

"Well, it seems that they contacted the Poles first

because they needed money and the Poles brought in the Russians."

"Why did they do that?"

She hesitated. "I'm not sure."

"Never mind. Have you seen the documents?"

"They're in the safe deposit at the Hilton, but I've seen one document."

He looked up quickly. "Tell me."

"I think most of the documents are copies—photostats—and they suspect that the papers may think they're fakes, so they've got one original. That's the one I've seen."

"What is it?"

"It's on White House paper and it's the minutes of a meeting between Roosevelt and Mackenzie King dated nineteen August 1940 and it has four paragraphs. It confirms that the meeting was held in the boardroom of Eastman Kodak in Rochester. That the Chiefs of Staff of both countries unanimously advised that it would be impossible to launch an invasion to liberate Europe without the United Kingdom as a fully operational base. That both leaders concurred and would inform Sir Winston Churchill to that effect and also inform him that if the Germans occupied any substantial part of the United Kingdom they would, after a few months, negotiate a treaty with the German Government."

"Signatures?"

"Yes, the President's and Mackenzie King's and a typewritten note saying that this was number two of two originals."

"Did it look genuine?"

"Yes, it looked very real to me."

He leaned back in his chair and looked at the ceiling, and after some moments of silence he sighed and said, "Where is it?"

"André Prouvost has it."

96

"Did he tell you all this?"

"Yes, he showed me the original when I said the papers wouldn't go for the photostats alone. The original is the crown jewel; the rest are just backup."

He stood up and walked around the desk and opened a small cupboard. He took out two glasses and held up a bottle of wine. "Château Margaux. Let's have a drink."

He poured the drink and then sat in the chair next to her. As he sipped he was thinking. As a last resort he'd relied on the Foreign Office and the White House being able to claim that the photostats were fakes. With the original the Frenchmen would have no problems. Any newspaper could check typefaces, paper, and Presidential movements overnight, and a couple of handwriting experts could confirm the signatures. It must be the Canadian original they'd got. Protocol would give seniority to the USA, and they'd have had number one. Involuntarily he shook himself like a dog coming out of water. "Where is it—the original?"

"Prouvost has it in a plain envelope, and he always keeps it on him."

"What did you feel about it all when he told you?"

"At first I couldn't believe it, but that document wasn't a fake, and although I know that it happened, I can't really take it in. All that's been said about the war, D-Day and all the rest of it, seems so phony now I know this. The minutes were so cold it was like seeing your father get the sack. I find that I just can't think about it —it makes me terribly angry but frightened at the same time. I'd almost like other people to know."

And that's just what others would feel too, thought Anders. Unbelieving, then frightened, then angry. The fact that there was almost no other way for the two governments to have acted would get swept aside unnoticed, like a log in a torrent of floodwater.

97

The girl spoke and cut across his thoughts. "I think the Frenchmen are being used by the Russians."

"How?"

"I don't know. They're not fools and they're tough in a way but they're not in the same league as the Russian. He's a professional, he's not a part-timer like them, and I don't think he'd be here if there wasn't even more to the operation than the exposure."

He put his hand on hers—"You're dead right, girl" —and he told her about the Russians' part of the plan.

When he'd finished she said, "My God, I'm quite sure the Frenchmen don't know about this part of it. People could get killed."

"People will get killed and there'll be demonstrations, protest strikes, American-owned firms will probably close down, and the Americans will leave Europe flat—no trade, no military support, nothing. Every country in Europe will suffer. All the old hatreds of Germany will be back and the Russians don't need to say a word. When they've lit the fuse they can sit back and wait. They won't need to wait for long; all their stooges in Europe will pay off at last." He stood up and stretched his arms. "Let's open another bottle."

They were halfway through the second bottle when the girl stood up. Still holding her glass, she bent over the rack of cassettes and looking at the titles picked one out. She half turned and said, "Can I put it on, Tad?"

He smiled. "Sure. What is it?"

She didn't answer, but a moment later lush violins were playing "La Mer," not Debussy's but Charles Trenet's.

She went on looking through the cassettes, and he was suddenly terribly aware of the long shapely legs and almost without thinking he was behind her and with a kind of inevitability his hand went under her arm and cupped her breast. For a few moments the girl said nothing as his fingers explored the firm flesh. Then she turned slowly and faced him. Her eyes were closed and she was trembling as she said, "Do you want me, Tad?"

His hands were gentle on her face and he said softly, "Open your eyes and look at me."

As they opened he kissed her mouth, and after a few moments she said, "Let's go to my room."

When she had taken off the white sweater she stood with her arms at her side so that he could see the full firm breasts. They looked even bigger naked and as his hands closed over them he bent to kiss her neck, and he groaned aloud as he saw the massive cluster of burn scars on her shoulder.

The girl clung to him fiercely. "Don't look, Tad, don't look. Just love me."

But he'd seen scars like those before, and he could feel the cigarettes burning his arm and his shoulder. Men had done it carefully and with the skill born of practice, ignoring her screams because they knew that in the end she'd talk. They must have gone on for a long time for the scars to be so many and so permanent.

He made love to her gently. Because he felt gentle. And as the night went on he realized that for the first time in his life he was really making love. It wasn't just technique, it wasn't just sex, it was a desperate need to make up for all the things that other men had done to this girl with the beautiful face and the sensuous body. It couldn't ever be done but it seemed to pacify them both.

With the new feeling of happiness and the desire to console and protect, Anders felt vulnerable himself. Part of his strength had gone. From now on he'd need emotional protection too, and only this girl would be able to give it. In the end she slept, but Tad bathed and dressed for a new day.

He took her for breakfast at Grosvenor House and told her how they would lay hands on the document. When she left he turned to wave as she walked down Park Lane toward the Hilton, and he would have been sad if he'd seen that she was crying. But he wouldn't have been able to do anything about it.

15

SOCIAL SCIENTISTS could probably supply the vital statistics that prove that there isn't a self-made millionaire who didn't start life selling newspapers. And there are certain locations that seem to supply a man with a patina of success. Half of downtown New York and more than half of the City of London wouldn't function or even exist if it wasn't for boys from Minsk and Warsaw, Budapest and Chicago. And if historical monuments were the catalysts of success, then Baltimore should be on the list. But it isn't. Even if it were, the lower end of Fayette Street would never be the launching site for millionaires. When you have a business down there, that's the best that's going to happen to you.

Federal agent Mendoza paused at the storefront window of a lower Fayette Street shop selling paperbacks and toys. When the shop was clear of customers he strolled in. The gray-haired old man behind the counter had a cup of coffee halfway to his mouth. He looked at Mendoza and long experience told him that this wasn't a customer. From the clothes and the hairstyle he was either from Equitable Life or the Hoover period of the FBI. He decided for FBI, and he lowered the coffee cup and said, "What can I do for you, chief?"

The badge in the man's palm confirmed the guess. "Are you Charles Parker?"

The old man shifted nervously. Pursing up his lips

in an attempt at a smile, he said, "I guess so—I'm Charlie Parker, all right."

"How much longer are you staying open?"

The old man squinted at the wall clock. "Fifteen—twenty minutes. Why, is anything wrong?"

"Mr. Parker, I've been instructed to bring you to Washington as soon as possible—tonight, that is."

The old man looked afraid. "Washington—tonight? I don't understand. I ain't got no business in Washington. Why, I never—"

The man interrupted. "Somebody in Washington wants your help, Mr. Parker. They'd like you there right now—and they've told me to drive you over. I gather you'll be paid for your trouble—and I'll wait for you and bring you back."

"But what's it all about? I don't know a damn soul in Washington, and I—"

"I don't know, Mr. Parker, I really don't know. How about I help you shut up shop?"

The old man was asleep when the car pulled up outside the big white building. Less than an hour later they were leaving, and Charlie Parker had received $2,000 in cash and a pat on the back from a man whose face he'd seen in the papers. He'd also signed the Oath of Secrecy and two famous signatures on a piece of crested paper. They'd told him what pens to use and left him on his own. The signatures were big florid scrawls—no trouble to Charlie at all. But he had never thought he'd live to see the day when they *paid* him to do it. Not after they'd given him ten years for doing much less. He had a little chuckle and settled back in the car.

For Joe DiBono Friday night was pizza night. The wife was visiting with her sisters and, as always on a Friday, she'd left three big pizzas for Joe and his cronies.

102

Joe was a poor card player, and poor card players, like good listeners, make plenty of friends. Tonight's gang were what the business magazines describe as "experience-based line-managers"; in other words, they could do their jobs with their eyes closed but they hadn't been to Harvard or MIT. Joe's wife had bought him a book for Christmas called *Poker as a Science* and he'd tried hard to understand it, but in the end he stuck to his well-tried and psychologically satisfying system—always bet on hearts and diamonds. There was something about those warm red cards that suited Joe's temperament.

They were well into the second pizza when the phone rang. "That'll be my old lady. You guys deal me in; I'll be right back." But it wasn't, and after a few seconds Joe was talking to a man whose name he had only seen on the glossy annual report that all IBM employees received. When he came back he bore bad news. "Boys, I've got to leave you—got to catch a plane in an hour. One of you'll have to pick up my wife and explain."

It was four hours later when Joe got to the main parts depot. He was taken straight to a large steel-clad vault. He stood by while the heavy steel doors were unlocked, unbolted, and swung open. There was row on row of steel shelves holding padlocked metal boxes clearly marked in white stencil with names like Pentagon, Secretary of State, US Navy, and SHAEF, and then there were two long shelves where every box was marked with the name of a President of the United States. There were a series of boxes marked F. D. Roosevelt, and Joe pulled out the one marked 1940 and laid it on the steel table. There was a file of invoices, statements, and receipts, a file of correspondence, and the rest of the box was lined with green baize and held a number of typewriter parts with small tie-on labels.

It took two hours in the machine shop and an hour's careful work with a senior man from Research before

Joe had finished. He handed over his work to the plant manager, who was waiting to take it to Washington.

When Joe arrived back home a boy was just delivering a bunch of roses to his wife. On the card it said, "Thanks for lending us the old man. Best regards, IBM."

The little American, who looked a bit like Harry Truman, spoke with a Texas accent and was full of enthusiasm for his subject. The two pieces of paper were lying at opposite ends of the small table, and between them was a magnifying glass on a stand, a micrometer, a finely graduated steel rule, a pair of dividers, and an infrared lamp. Tad listened carefully to what the man was saying.

"Well now, Mr. Anders, can *you* tell which one's the original?"

Anders looked at both pages and then used the magnifying glass, but there was no difference that he could see.

He shook his head, and the wiry little man said, "I've prepared a written and notarized report on the substitute document, and it's been filed with your colleague at the Foreign Office, Mr. Kent."

"That's fine, Mr. Lake, but I'd like to go over the points with you again. I don't know how technical they are, but I'd appreciate a briefing."

"Of course, Mr. Anders. Let's go over it point by point. First things first: paper. The substitute is slightly but measurably thicker. If it was examined by paper experts, they would confirm that it couldn't possibly be more than five years old. It looks as old as the original but its contents are much too modern to have been around in 1939 when the original paper was made. We've folded the substitute exactly like the original and the laboratory has applied dust particles so that the crease marks look the same in both.

"Now we come to the typing, and we've introduced a number of differences here. We've been able to use the same type face exactly, but we've used a golf-ball head; that means that the depth of impression is much greater. The President's secretary never used a golf-ball head. In fact it wasn't much more than a vague research project until the war was over. Both letters are seemingly double-spaced between the lines but they are in fact spaced differently. Fortunately we've still got FDR's typewriter in our museum, so a comparison could easily be made.

"In the printing, the address here has been moved five millimeters to the left. You can't see it but you can measure it easily. And finally the design of the crest has been altered in two places—here on the eagle's claw and here in the wing feathers." He looked up at Anders and grinned. "We're pleased with it, Mr. Anders, very pleased."

Anders had booked into the room next to the girl and they'd waited at the Hilton for two days before the call came. The Frenchmen were all down at the house at Temple now, but André Prouvost was impatient to see the girl and Anders had guessed that sooner or later he'd contact her. When the girl put down the telephone she said, "Well, he's coming for the night. He'll be here abut eight o'clock."

Anders nodded. "OK—now remember he's got to be pretty drunk already before you fix his drink or he'll be suspicious when he wakes up."

Back in his own room next door, Anders slid off his jacket and then took out the envelope. He unfolded the letter once again and was pleased with the job they'd done. It went back into the inside pocket of his jacket. It was nearly eight thirty when he heard the doorbell ring next door, and there were voices but he couldn't make out what was said. He read the previous day's report from the surveillance team at the lockkeeper's cottage. They had abandoned an attempt on the house tonight to try and examine the cases from the lorry.

Anders pulled back the curtain and looked out on Park Lane and Hyde Park Corner. The lights glittered and sparkled and London was going about its evening business. He felt lonely because of the inaction. Everyone else had something to do, but he was only waiting. When it was all over he'd take the girl away and they'd have some weeks of sunshine and rest. They could rent an apartment in Portofino or Santa Margherita. And in his mind's eye they were walking up the hill at Santa Margherita, past white garden walls and overhanging trees weighed down with figs or peaches. It was hot, and the road was dusty, and they'd soon be with *il professore*, sitting in the shade in his garden, sipping Asti Spumanti and looking over the red and orange-tiled roofs, down to the bay and the fishing boats at the jetty. They'd talk and argue mildly about Italian politics or La Lollo and the girl would feel safe and secure.

There were two knocks on the communicating door and he glanced at his watch. It was past midnight. He stood to the side of the door, his hand across his chest and around the butt of the pistol under his left armpit. The handle turned slowly, and then the door opened and the girl was standing there. She was naked except for her sweater, which was pulled up to expose her breasts. She was pale and her eyes were dull. She looked at his face and said, "He's out now," and stood aside to let him go inside her room.

He noticed the empty bottles of wine and the cigarette butts and the man lying back in the chair, his head on his shoulder and his legs sprawled out. He was wearing only a bathrobe. Anders stood behind the chair and listened to his breathing. It was shallow but even, and when he pulled back one eyelid the pupil was dilated and the man didn't move.

106

The jacket was on the bed, and as his hand slid into the inner pocket he felt the envelope. He took it out, removed the letter, examined it, and then walked through to his own room and placed it in the hand basin in the bathroom. He took the substitute letter, slid it into the envelope, and replaced it in the jacket pocket. He washed both the empty wine glasses thoroughly in the bathroom and then partly filled them both from the half-empty wine bottle, and closed the door quietly as he went back to his own room.

The girl was standing by the window looking out. Her back was golden from the bedside lamp, but her face and the front of her body were almost silver from the moonlight. He sensed that she didn't want to be disturbed and went into the bathroom. He took a last look at the original document and then lit one corner and held it as it burned up to his finger and thumb. The last small triangle he burned on a pin. He ran the basin full of warm water, and the charred paper slowly became particles of dust that turned the water gray. They no longer had substance. He let the gray matter run out and left both taps running for several minutes.

When he walked into the room, the girl was still there but she'd removed the sweater. He realized she'd left on the sweater to cover the giveaway burns on her arm and shoulder. The Frenchman would have been suspicious. Major Tad Anders' thinking was impeccable; nevertheless it was wrong.

When Anders had gone the girl went back to her own room and dressed. The Frenchman woke at six. He wasn't suspicious and he phoned the others to say he would be back in an hour, and then he was in a hurry to get on his way.

Ten minutes later the girl left the hotel and walked across St. James's Park, along the Mall, and then through to Westminster Bridge. She walked to the South Bank where it approaches the Festival Hall and sat on a bench looking over the Thames. She could see traffic moving on the Embankment, and Big Ben struck a solemn half hour for eight thirty. It seemed hard to believe that this same river flowed past the Mill House at Temple. She wondered where it all would end. When Anders had first made love to her it was the first time since the prison in Saigon. Before Anders she had always known that if she slept with a man she would be back in the nightmare of brutality when men took turns to have her and then fought each other to have her again. Before she'd become unconscious all she could remember was the purple bougainvillaea around the small window, lit by the hot sun outside the dark room where her countrymen used her body. Until Anders, no man apart from doctors had even seen the scars on her shoulders and arm. They were too private, and she would never be able to say the words to explain them away. No ordinary man would understand her feelings; she couldn't understand them herself. But she had known Anders was different. He was in the racket and he'd understand the feelings of revulsion and defeat; she'd sensed his own scars and watched them at work. She had known he understood. She had hated the arranged seduction of the Frenchman, but because it was for Anders she wouldn't let it hurt. Anders too enjoyed the big firm breasts and the space between her thighs, but she knew he hadn't made love just for that. Their life and their training made them know about people, and she knew about Anders and she cared and loved, but she knew it could bring disaster to them both if they relaxed before this work was over.

When she got back to the hotel the Russian was waiting for her.

16

THE LAST LIGHT went out in the Mill House just before midnight. Anders waited for another two hours on the boat before making any move. There were ducks roosting along the riverbank so he moved over cautiously to the gravel path through the trees and stood silently under the giant cedar and watched the house. The moon shone on the upper windows, but the ground floor was hidden by the high brick wall. There were no lights in the lockkeeper's cottage, but he knew that someone would be on watch.

There were no gates at the wide entrance in the wall, just high brick pillars with weathered stone lions and massive hinges for the wrought-iron gates that had probably gone during the war years. The white Jag was parked facing the gates, ready to go, and Anders noted subconsciously that they were not being careless. He walked slowly along a finger of shadow from one of the outbuildings that took him within a stride of the house. He injected a squirt of oil in the keyhole on the big front door and waited for a few moments before easing in the key. It turned easily, and when he'd closed the door behind him he stood silent and still, just inside the hall. The moonlight showed up the white palladian columns, and after a few minutes his eyes adjusted and he could make out the door of the room with the boxes. In the quiet of the night the house creaked and groaned as the old wood reacted to the dry heat of the central heating, but there was no other sound from upstairs.

The lock on the door had been changed, but the replacement responded to the adjustable skeleton key and the door creaked only slightly as he opened it slowly. In the bright moonlight he could see that there were two long narrow boxes and four square crates. None of them was locked. In the first of the boxes he loosened the burlap wrapping and the greaseproof paper and carried the gun to the light from the window. It was an SLR, FN, the latest Belgian model made at the Fabrique Nationale d'Armes de Guerre. It was one of the most advanced automatic weapons currently available for the services, firing at a rate of up to 700 rounds a minute. There was oil glistening on the working parts and the barrel was assembled, but there was no magazine fitted. He estimated that there were ten rifles in the box. The second box confirmed his estimate. There were dozens of 60-round magazines, all loaded, and a few 20-round staggered-box magazines and rows of 5-round clips. There were exactly ten infrared sighting devices, and he knew that these were undergoing NATO proving tests and were still on secret classification. There were about 30,000 rounds all told.

The four square crates were marked with the name of a well-known British engineering company, but Anders wasn't surprised at the contents. In the first there was row on row of neatly packed detonators. Reels of light wire. Craftsman-built timing devices. All the other crates had explosives only, ranging from dynamite to superplastic. There was enough explosive in the room to wipe out a fair-sized town. The Frenchmen were certainly in on the whole operation, not just the news break. Anders wedged a small white piece of plastic between two of the wooden slats. It was about ½ inch by ¼ inch and no thicker than a postcard. There was nearly 100 feet of microcircuit in the thin plastic. Put to another use, the technology would have produced a good radio receiver about the size of a shirt button.

When he was back on the boat, Anders phoned the house in Hampshire and the team at the lockkeeper's cottage. They hadn't seen him arrive at the house, but they had seen him leaving as he passed in front of the white Jag.

The Russian had been sitting in the Hilton foyer, and when he saw the girl arrive he went to the lift and waited for her. When she saw him she stopped. The big handsome face was smiling but the eyes were like animal's eyes, observing but not commenting.

"M'selle Foubert, I hoped I'd be fortunate enough to find you here."

"Oh—why?"

"I wanted to talk with you. Maybe we should have more privacy in your room."

She half smiled and shook her head. "Let's go up to the lounge, Mr. Eklund."

When they were seated together in the corner he wasted no time. "What do you think of young Prouvost?"

She raised her eyebrows. "I never gossip, Mr. Eklund." To soften the snub, she said, "Not even among friends."

But he wasn't that easily snubbed. He flipped his hand and shrugged. "How's your work going along?"

"Not too badly, but I'm mainly here for a rest."

The Russian got back to the subject again. "The others are very annoyed with Prouvost. I understand he spent the night with you without permission."

He was looking intently at her and she stared back. "Whose permission?"

He didn't respond. "We don't want him to come to

any harm—or you, for that matter," he added, and looked to see how she'd take it.

She drew a deep breath. "You're being offensive, Mr. Eklund," and she made to get up. He put his hand on her wrist, smiling, but the grip on her wrist was like a padlock and she had to sit down.

"M'selle Foubert, we think you know too much. Prouvost talked too much. So what are we going to do?"

She didn't speak.

His eyes were like those of a bird of prey, penetrating and finely alert. "How much did he tell you?"

"Why don't you ask him?"

"I have."

"So?"

"So we've dealt with him, but that still leaves you."

He let go of her wrist and leaned back in his chair. He was worried because she didn't appear to be frightened, and most women would be. Most men would be too.

She cut across his thoughts. "Mr. Eklund, I'm going to leave you now, and if you make any move to stop me I'll shout the place down."

He looked at her unsmiling and said, "You do what you please, ma'm'selle, but you'd be wiser to talk with me now. It could save us all a lot of trouble."

She stood up, patted down her skirt, nodded to him, and walked off through to the foyer. He made no move to follow her, but she'd seen the look in his eyes. He wasn't used to being thwarted.

It was nearly ten minutes later when her phone rang. She listened for almost three minutes before she hung up. Prouvost's screams were ringing in her ears. They were real enough. She'd heard screams like those before. Some had been hers. But all he had said between the sobs and the agony was, "Do what they say—for God's sake do what they say!"

Her hand was on the phone to ring Anders when there was a knock on the door. She had no doubt who it was, and when she opened it the Russian was standing there. One hand was in his jacket pocket, but it wasn't to keep it warm. She looked at him for a moment and then said quietly, "You'd better come in."

He pushed the door flat against the wall and then closed it. He looked behind curtains and under the bed, checked the bathroom, and walked over to the window and looked out. Then he went carefully through the drawers in the dressing table, the writing desk, and the clothes in the wardrobe. Finally he opened her bag and tipped out its contents. He spent a long time on her passport, especially on the pages of visa stamps. He looked across at her. "What were you doing in Saigon?"

"Working for Agence France Presse."

"Doing what?"

"Reporting on the war."

He threw the passport down on the table and turned on the radio. She guessed he was still wondering if the room was bugged. He sat down and waved her to the other chair. "What did you think of the Frenchmen's scheme?"

"Stupid."

"Why?"

"No experienced editor's going to print photostats —they'll need better than that."

He looked at her speculatively and decided she didn't know about the original. "Why did you choose London for your rest?"

She gave a typical Parisian shrug. "Cheap—I don't know it at all—not far to come."

"What do you think of the English?"

Another Gallic shrug. "I've hardly met any. André took most of my time." He smiled and she reluctantly smiled with him.

He turned his face as if he were looking out of the window, but his eyes were turned to watch her face. "How'd you like to help me?"

"I'm not really interested. It seems a lot of schoolboy stuff to me."

"We'd pay you well."

She shook her head, but she knew he'd have to involve her or kill her.

"Say a nice fox coat."

She looked interested, and with a smile she said, "Siberian fox?"

His eyes narrowed. "The Frenchman told you about me?"

She nodded. He swore in Russian and stood up. "I just want you to look at some buildings with me."

She smiled. "Ah, the pretty girl used as a diversion."

"What makes you think that?"

"It's an old, old journalist's trick."

"What about it, then?"

She stood up. "Full-length fox coat, then."

He grinned and held out the big crushing hand. "It's a deal."

He arranged to meet her the next morning.

The police inspector, who had been well briefed, said, "I'm afraid it isn't a pleasant sight, Your Excellency," and turned down the covering sheet. Borowski looked at Krezki's waxen, bruised face and after a few moments said, "How did it happen, officer?"

"Well, we'll be giving you an official report, sir, but as far as we can tell he was hit by a car. A taxi, one of the witnesses said."

"Will you prosecute?"

"Pretty unlikely, sir. Nobody really saw what happened, and the cabbie probably doesn't know he hit anybody. It was very dark at the time."

"Where did it happen?"

The Inspector fished in an inside pocket and brought out a notebook. "Seems like it was in Grosvenor Road, sir. It runs alongside the river in Pimlico."

There was a piece in the Slough *Evening Mail*.

The body of a man was discovered in the Thames by two early-morning anglers today. A police spokesman told our reporter that foul play was not suspected but they appealed for anyone who might have any information to contact them at Reading. The body, which has been recovered from the river, was that of a man in his middle or late thirties, and it was discovered by Mr. Alfred Wheeler and his eldest son John near the weir at Marsh Lock upriver from Henley. Mr. Wheeler told our reporter that the body and face had been extensively bruised. Local residents say that they have complained to the Rural District Council on many occasions about the lack of fencing around the weir. Col. Stephenson, chairman of the RDC, told us that the matter would certainly be discussed at next month's council meeting but it had already been established that suitable fencing could cost up to £75, a considerable burden on the ratepayers.

Anders' surveillance team at the lockkeeper's cottage had watched the Frenchmen put Prouvost's body into the back of the Jag, and the small transmitter behind the radiator grille had given them and Security Signals a fix long before the Jag had stopped at Marsh Lock. The local village policeman had quietly watched as the body had been carried through the high fronds of mace and cow parsley that fringed the riverbank at Marsh Lock. He had not seen the body put in the water but he had watched the three men return to the Jag and drive off. It went against his policeman's instincts to do nothing, but he carried out his instructions and telephoned his report to the Chief Superintendent at Reading.

The tall, thin man was definitely tailing her, and the girl told the taxi to stop at Simpson's. While she was paying the cabbie she could see without moving her head that the man was paying off his taxi about thirty yards farther along Piccadilly on the same side. She went through the shop to the phone booths, and as she dialed she could see him strolling around the display of hand-bags and travel goods. Then she was speaking quietly to Anders.

"Tad, I can't make it to your place. I'm being tailed."

"Why were you coming here?"

"The Russian's trying to recruit me."

"What as?"

"As a distraction to go around with him— the usual female role. But they've beaten up Prouvost and I think the Russian can't make his mind up about me. Would like to wipe me out but doesn't quite know what the repercussions would be."

"Give me a description of the tail."

She went down him from hair to shoes.

"Where is he now?"

"I'm at Simpson's near the travel goods section."

There was a long pause. Then he said, "Right, now listen carefully. Get a taxi and go to the Royal Court Theatre in Sloane Square. Pay him off. If the theatre booking office is open, buy a ticket for any day next week. If it's closed, just look surprised and confused. There'll be two taxis parked by the theater. Take the first one and he'll take you back to the Hilton. Phone me from your room in two hours' time. Take it all slowly and have a good look around Simpson's or he'll know you only went in to phone, and I need some time to fix things. *Sois sage, minouche.*" And he hung up. She held the phone to her ear for a few moments to enjoy the thought of the last few words.

The man bought a paper outside Sloane Square tube station, and when the girl came down the theater steps putting something in her handbag he saw her speak to the taximan, who nodded as she spoke, and the girl stepped in. He didn't look at the taxi as it passed him but gave a pound note to the driver of the second taxi and said, "Follow that taxi, please. Don't lose it." He got in, the driver moved a lever under the fascia board, pulled down the hire flag, and drove off. The taxis parted company at Battersea Bridge and the tall, thin man shouted and banged to no avail. When he tried the doors neither of them would open.

When the taxi driver closed the big double gates, the tall, thin man saw the sign that said STUDIO JASON. He kept his left hand on the gun in his pocket. When the taxi driver went inside the building, the tall, thin man moved the catch to safety on the gun and holding the barrel hammered it hard on the windows. The fiber side panels on the grip split apart but the windows stayed undamaged. Then there was a faint sweet smell of hyacinths, and two minutes later the man was quiet and still, his head lolling forward and his body leaning against the door.

When the unconscious tail had been carried in, Anders had picked up the pistol and the broken side panels from the floor of the taxi. He sat playing with the pistol, waiting for the man to recover. It was a 9 mm Makarov pistol, a crib of the German Walther PP, a dangerous crib for anyone not used to it because it looked exactly like a Walther, but the safety catch worked the opposite way round. Anders pulled down the trigger guard, pulled the slide back and up, and let the recoil spring slide off the barrel. He assembled it again but without the spring and locked it in the wall safe.

When the man came to he was in the special room and Anders was sitting facing him. Anders didn't speak; he just looked at the man's face. When the pupils of the man's eyes were almost back to normal, he started.

117

"What's your name?"

The man shook his head and smiled.

But when Anders said, "*Kak nazywajesia?*" the man's face drained of blood and he went to get up. Anders pushed him back into the chair and said it again. That Anders spoke in Russian was the man's only clue. He had heard of these situations before, where an apparat became suspect or one part of the KGB eliminated another and the operators never knew why, except that they must be working for a loser. He looked at Anders' face and there were all the trademarks of the successful KGB man, and he wondered who'd given him the fresh lacerations down the side of his face. Then suddenly Anders' hand was in the man's hair and his head was jerked back till he could hardly breathe and Anders asked him his name again.

"Komlosy."

"Who are you working for?"

The man was trembling violently because he suspected his time was nearly up.

"Rudenko."

"Why were you tailing the girl?"

"He wanted to check on her."

"Where are you based here?"

"Highgate."

"At the Trade Mission house?"

"Yes."

"What's your cover?"

"Sales of photographic stuff—cameras and accessories."

"Who do you normally operate for?"

"Apparat Seven."

"Doing what?"

"I'm one of the cutouts."

"When do you report next to Rudenko?"

The man looked at his watch. "Half an hour ago."

Anders questioned the man for another hour and then went into his own office and picked up the phone. "Sneddon? This is Tad Anders. I've dredged up a Russian named Komlosy. I've finished with him but he worked for one of the KGB apparats. He was borrowed for another KGB operation and we picked him up. I don't want him any more, but I'd guess he's got quite a lot of stuff that could interest you. D'you want him?" Anders listened carefully. "OK. Well, you send for him. He's at my place, but when you've done with him that's the end of the line for him—is that understood?" He shook his head in irritation as he listened, and finally he snapped. "You don't need any authority, Sneddon, beyond mine. Now listen, if you want to interrogate this guy you'll have to do it over here. I'll deal with him afterwards. The longest you've got is twenty-four hours." And he slammed down the phone. Anders was getting just a little bit ragged at the edges.

17

THE GIRL HAD LOOKED at her watch a dozen times
in as many minutes and there were still ten minutes to
go before she was to phone Anders. There was a
knock on the door and she jumped up quickly and flung
it open. The Russian was leaning against the doorframe,
not in relaxation but to mask the gun he was holding in
his left hand. He kicked the door open and walked in.
The girl backed away until her legs were against the
divan bed. She sat down and he watched every move
she made as he closed the door.

"Pack your things—everything."

"Why?"

She ducked but his open hand smashed against the
side of her head and the floor sloped away and she fell
back half conscious on the bed. Then his hand snatched
at the top of her sweater and pulled her into a sitting position. As the mist cleared from her eyes she saw the
burning anger on his face, and when he ground out,
"Pack it all—quickly," it didn't need the wave of the
gun to make her obey. She wondered what had caused
the outburst and hoped that Anders might phone before
she left. But he didn't.

The Russian stayed close behind her while she paid
her bill and then carried her case with one hand; the gun
in the other was covered by her coat. A chauffeured car
with diplomatic plates drew across the entrance as they

walked out. The chauffeur took her cases and helped her into the car, followed by the Russian. An hour and a half later they pulled up at the house at Temple.

Igor Rudenko was an experienced operator, and when the tail had not reported back to him two hours after the arranged time he had done a little arithmetic. When he'd added the defector from the *Batory* to the death of Krezki and Komlosy's failure to report, he didn't like the answer and he had an instinct that the operation was leaking. Prouvost had endangered the Frenchmen with the girl, and the tail he'd put on her was only routine—but now the tail had disappeared his suspicions were aroused.

Anders phoned the girl at the Hilton but there was no reply. He checked with reception and was told she had checked out nearly two hours ago. He had hardly put the phone back in its cradle when the radio operator came in and handed him a report from the surveillance unit at the lockkeeper's cottage. A car identified as Russian Embassy from Kensington had arrived fifteen minutes ago. Mlle. Foubert and several bags had been handed over to the two Frenchmen. She had been escorted inside the house by Firette and there had been an angry scene between Rudenko and Loussier, during which Rudenko had grabbed the Frenchman by his jacket and shoved him against the car. The chauffeur had not interfered, and eventually Rudenko had got back in the car and left.

Anders was sure that if the Frenchmen or the Russian had seen the girl as anything more than a possible accidental leak because of what Prouvost had told her in his amorous ramblings she would have been killed rather than removed. Also, they were probably not sure what repercussions there would be to her death. They were uncertain of her importance. She'd been seen as a casual pickup, but missing girls, especially pretty ones, always cause a stink when they go missing, and Rudenko had ignored usual security precautions and called in a car from the embassy; he couldn't wait for a car from Highgate or some other source. It could make them speed up the operation. There was some slight additional protection for the girl that Anders could provide. If he tried to spring her from the house at Temple they'd know for certain she was dangerous, but he could pressure them with some publicity about her.

Anders had been to Room 1501 at the Hilton in case the girl had been able to leave some message or clue as to what was happening, but there was nothing. And now Anders was sitting with the deputy manager of the Hilton, who was making the phone call to the French Embassy. It had taken the persuasion of the US Ambassador to get the deputy manager to do it. He spoke good French, and when the call was made he asked for the Third Secretary. A few moments later he was through.

"Ah, Monsieur Thierry, how are you? . . . Just a small matter that I felt I should mention to you personally. One of my managers was at the reception desk yesterday when a young lady was paying her bill. . . . No, it's not a question of fraud. . . . Yes, you see he was a bit worried that she seemed to be under some sort of pressure. There was a man with her apparently. . . . Ah, yes, I see. Well, I felt you should know because the young lady was one of your nationals. . . . Yes, of course, it was a Mlle. Marie-Claire Foubert. . . . Yes, a Paris address, Rue de la Croix twenty-seven, Sixteenth Arrondissement. I see. . . . Of course. . . . No, we have no details of the man, but the doorman says they went off together in one of the Soviet Embassy cars."

He was listening carefully and nodded his head to Anders, and finally after some pleasantries he hung up.

"So, Mr. Anders, was that what you wanted?"

"Absolutely first class. What did he say?"

"Oh, at first not interested at all, but when I told him about the car he was obviously in a hurry to finish the call and do some checking. I got the impression that he's not going to the police."

"You've briefed the doorman and one of your managers?"

The deputy manager nodded and stood up. "Of course. Mr. Anders, I carried out your wishes, and now, if you'll excuse me, I'll get back to running the hotel."

There was a folder of reports on Anders' desk when he got back, and he read them through carefully. There was the routine monitoring of radio and telephone traffic at the house in the Avenue Foch and a long report, with photographs and a videotape spool, from the team at the lockkeeper's cottage. A routine report from Central Intelligence covering the previous day's comings and goings at the Highgate house. Rudenko had paid brief visits there the last three days. There was a report from the British Embassy in Moscow that the military attaché had received a hint from a Red Army contact that his contacts with the KGB were not welcomed and that if they continued he would be classified as *persona non grata*. There was a note attached to this report by the First Secretary pointing out that it was most unusual for any Red Army source to interfere with casual embassy contacts with the KGB and quite unknown for any diplomatic threat to come from the army. There had been an intercept two days ago of a signal from Moscow to Rudenko in the Snowball code to operate phase two immediately. Macdonald in Paris reported that the Polish explosives expert from Z-11 had left the house in Avenue Foch and had flown via BEA to London. Special Branch had identified him at Heathrow, and he had been followed to a house in Chiswick. He was now under permanent surveillance.

There was a report from Port Security that four men had gone ashore from the Russian fishing vessel *Pyotr Illych*, which was undergoing repair at Cardiff, and had not returned. There was a courtesy extract from the US National Security Agency monitoring station in Wales that a Soviet submarine had rendezvoused with a large fishing vessel off Fishguard. The NSA had identified the submarine as the K-97, a Sverdlovsk-class vessel used for long-range surveillance. The K-97 had maintained twelve hours' radio silence before and after the rendezvous but had been positively identified by her diesel engine signal pattern. Two of the men from the *Pyotr Illych* had been identified as KGB men previously used in the Republic of Ireland. All four had traveled to London and they had separately been followed to a shop in Shepherd's Market, a boardinghouse near Victoria Station, a country cottage near Oxford, and a house in Birmingham. Separate full-time surveillance had been mounted on Anders' instructions.

Anders had just hung up from the last of a string of telephone calls when he was brought the first edition of the next day's *Daily Express*. The headlines were about rumors of a snap General Election, but right on the front page was a piece about a missing French girl journalist and a possible link with an Iron Curtain embassy. It wasn't big and it didn't say much, but the embassy would spot it all right and it would be some insurance for the girl. He made one more phone call before he went to bed, and it was a long time before he slept. He dreamed of a woman with a bouquet waving from a big car. She was smiling with tears in her eyes, and as it faded he saw it was Marie-Claire Foubert.

He was reading the overnight reports by 6 A.M. the next morning and in the general report on unidentified radio traffic someone had underlined a report on faint transmissions in the Thames valley on a shortwave frequency sometimes used by SIS. The signals had been spasmodic from 2300 hours on the previous day to 0300 hours this morning. The matter was further confused by the fact that whoever was operating the transmitter was using a low-grade marine distress call and some as yet unidentified code. Whoever had underlined the extract had obviously wondered if Thames valley might indicate some transmission by the Frenchmen at Temple. There had been no signal traffic from the house up to now. And then the red light flashed and he remembered the small transmitter he had given the girl right at the start. She had been amused because it was the type of radio much used by SDECE in France. The housing was a genuine container for a Lancôme lipstick and the tiny radio gave a good signal over a ten-mile radius. Anders had notified Signals Security of the wavelength allocated to the girl and possible transmission area. Because it had not been used before, it had probably been classified as "not in use." Twenty minutes later he was in his signals control room, and tapes of the "suspect and unidentified" transmissions were called up. Anders smiled when he heard them and remembered Macdonald's notes in Paris. No wonder the girl had failed her radio courses. The Morse was hesitant and jerky with long gaps. She was using the marine distress call PAN as her call sign and it wasn't in code. It was bad Morse in French. She was notifying her location. There was no way he could contact her because there were no receiving facilities on the girl's radio. He played one of the tapes to Mac in Paris, who confirmed and identified the girl's hesitant Morse.

By midday her signal had been reported by a Port of London Authority patrol boat as an improper use of the PAN call sign, which was only for ships and aircraft in distress. They in turn had been given a flea in their ears through the Postmaster General for monitoring signals not in the marine bands. The Russian monitoring unit in Kensington had picked up a weak signal in French and dismissed it as an amateur because of the marine call sign being used inland; it was logged as probably a test transmission from a Thames pleasure craft. A US National Security Agency monitoring unit near Grosvenor Square picked it up and sent it back to HQ in the States, who referred it to the CIA, who discussed it for four hours, had a good guess at what it might be, and their liaison officer in London fed it back as a sign of goodwill to SIS, who ground their teeth a little at Anders' operation using inefficient amateur operators. They made some technical recommendations to him but there was nothing he could do. He felt as if the whole world was listening in, but the girl's transmissions were useful insurance. The signal he got late that night was worth all the trouble. It was brief; it just said PAN PAN PAN BIG MEETING TOMORROW NOT ME MINOUCHE.

18

In Moscow after three days of cold sunshine the weather had changed and was now typical of early October in the city. The sky was overcast and there was a wind that called for overcoats and hats. The old man who stepped out of the Zim buttoned up his coat and turned his face from the wind and held onto his hat. Colonel Gouzenko had a reputation as a man of brawn rather than brain, but he'd survived all the purges and infighting since the war had finished. Some said it was because he had only had two promotions in thirty years, and others that he was much brighter than the bright boys of the KGB and the GRU. They were too political for most of the soldiers, and it was Colonel Gouzenko's official duty to act as liaison with both the KGB and the GRU on matters that could affect the army.

Foreigners never really grasped the role of the Soviet Army. They saw marshals and generals and colonels executed or disgraced and they saw the Party as the master of all Russia, but it wasn't so and from 1953 onward never had been. Those who were disposed of were generally the army's outcasts rather than the politicians' victims. A strong man doesn't need to hit out to prove his strength, and the Red Army had stood back like a giant and watched the politicians fret and contrive their

127

little five-year stints of power and publicity. Nothing was written and little was said, but all the protagonists knew where the parameters of power were drawn. The army had only two tasks—to defend Russia and control every inch of the earth's surface they could master. And for Russia you couldn't substitute the Communist Party— the generals could brush the Party away like a man flicking crumbs from a table. Since Khrushchev the Party had been an instrument of the army, even if it looked the other way around to Western eyes, and the army wasn't worried about appearances; it knew its business better than the politicians knew theirs. There was a time when the balance was almost even, but not enough politicians died fighting between 1940 and 1945, and they had been paying that debt ever since, and they would pay it for decades to come. The Russian people silently and subconsciously watched and listened and noted that it was politicians who backed away in Cuba, Berlin, China, Africa, and the Mediterranean. And it was politicians who had backed away in 1945 when the Red Army could have rolled to the Channel ports in a week, against its exhausted Allies.

One of the regiments recently transferred to Moscow from the frontier with China was guarding the Lubyanka complex that housed the central offices of the KGB. Gouzenko returned the guard's salute formally and correctly, but as he was walking up the steps something caught his eye and he went back. The soldier looked ahead but was conscious of the colonel examining his rifle. A few moments later Gouzenko was asking for the guard commander. He was a young lieutenant, and he took in Gouzenko's rows of medals and guessed he wasn't KGB. When the colonel looked him in the eye he put up his chin and was stiffly at attention.

"Name, comrade?"

"Lieutenant Tomarov, comrade colonel, B Company, Fifteenth Assault Regiment guard commander, sir."

"Why are your guards armed with sniper's rifles?"

"Those are our current issue, sir."

The Dragunov was a first-class, up-to-date, sniper's rifle. It could rip out almost 900 rounds in a minute but it was a sniper's weapon with a model PSO-1 scope sight. It also had an unusual stock with a large cutout to the rear of the pistol grip. And all these curlicues meant that a man couldn't hold it on his shoulder on guard without tangling it up in his shoulder straps and pockets. It could take him at least a minute before he could open fire, and a minute is a long time. The standard weapon for Lubyanka guards was the Simonov carbine, but somebody had been lazy and inefficient. Nothing ever happened outside the Lubyanka so people got careless, and this unit had been in Moscow for two days and nobody had bothered to withdraw the assault weapons and issue SKS carbines. It was laxity like this that could eat into an army and destroy it.

"Lieutenant Tomarov, you will report to GHQ Moscow Defense to Major Bross. You will give him my compliments and tell him I want a full report—in writing—of who is responsible for this gross breach of standing orders, and he will bring the report to me here, together with your battalion commander."

"Sir." And Tomarov clicked his heels and saluted.

Gouzenko was not impressed and turned away with irritation and stamped up the stone steps and across the tiled hall to the wide, sweeping staircase.

The room he entered was large and high-ceilinged with ornate and old-fashioned decorations on carved wood panels, silk wall coverings, and light from three crystal chandeliers. The windows were high and narrow with deep red tapestry curtains, the carpet was Bokhara, and the beautiful long table had been in one of the

Czar's seaside homes. There were several comfortable large armchairs arranged around a low glass coffee table, on whose top was a bowl of fruit and a tray of nuts and chocolate creams.

There were two men at one of the windows and they turned as Gouzenko entered. The man who was standing was Yessov, a KGB civilian and very senior, and the other was Georg Levin, a colonel in the GRU. Yessov was holding a glass of pale white wine and Levin had been lighting a thin cigar.

There was an old-fashioned wooden coat and hat rack in an alcove beside the door and Gouzenko hung up his uniform coat and hat, and with a glance at the other two he took off his leather belt and hung it loosely with his gloves. It wasn't an army mess, but he liked the little courtesies like taking off sidearms and belt as a sign of relaxation and good manners. He walked over to the window and nodded to Yessov, whom he despised.

The KGB saw themselves as the avant-garde, the setters of new standards, and Yessov was typical of the new-style KGB director. He had been successful in America, Canada, and France and had handled the rather tangled arrangements for the Englishmen Burgess and Maclean from the moment they had decided to leave the West. He reckoned he was a mile smarter than Gouzenko but he didn't underrate the old tiger's influence. Those icy gray eyes could be quite daunting at times, as if they knew something you didn't know that was going to head you to the Undeveloped Territories. Nikita Gouzenko was the Soviet Army personified, and Yessov had seen him and his fellow officers watching in the past six years. They seldom aired their views outside their own tight circles but they were remarkably clued in on everything that went on. They all seemed a hundred years old, with a wisdom that was almost a reflex; they were like some Russian proverbs, corny but all too often proved right.

Yessov jerked his glass. "How about some for you, Nikita?"

Gouzenko looked easily and without smiling into the self-satisfied face. "When we've finished, Yessov—if the news is good."

Yessov put down his foot from the window seat and smiling at Levin he said, "Looks like we'd better get started, Levin." He waved toward the armchairs. "I've had them set out the coffee table for us." He moved over with an air of authority. After all, it was KGB headquarters and he was host and they were guests. And what was better, the news was good, and the generals hadn't looked far enough ahead. When Operation Snowball was finished the army could be cut in half because the politicians would have shown how to conquer the world without troops. The big brown bear could be given a pot of honey and a pat on its shaggy back while its master took over.

The three men settled in the armchairs but Gouzenko still managed to look military and sat leaning alertly forward, his hands clasped between his knees. He listened without comment while Yessov read out the various reports and brought them up to date on the operation.

It was nearly an hour later when Yessov finished and put down the thick file on the low table. "All we've got to decide is when we tell Rudenko to press the button. Have either of you got any views?"

Levin lit another cigarette, and as he leaned back he said, "Ambassador Borowski's report says that it's his opinion that the news that the Americans and the Canadians would have made a deal with the Nazis is going to cause some annoyance, but it may not amount to anything more."

"Ambassador Borowski doesn't know most of the operation. He's just considering the original plan the Frenchmen cooked up. That's only the starting gun."

Levin pursed his lips. "The other thing in my mind is that Rudenko is promising quite a lot. How much is guaranteed and how much is wishing?"

Yessov picked up the file and went through the top papers and pulled out a couple of foolscap sheets and read them while the others sat silent. Then he looked up. "This is an analysis by the director of Apparat Seven in Britain—and he's no lover of Rudenko, as you'll have gathered from previous reports. Just going down the certainties we've got a pretty good picture. In week one the press revelations and several thousand letters to editors to show public indignation. By the end of the week there's the first lot of pieces suggesting that the Americans are still exploiting their old allies. In week two there are mass meetings of protest in London and seven provincial centers, plus two certain discussion programs on TV with an analysis of the effects on sterling inflation of the dollar crisis. And a paperback listing American interest or ownership of industrial and commercial concerns in Britain." He looked at Levin and Gouzenko. "In fact it's a pretty damaging position, and when you start naming names it's going to be very hard to defend. Anyway, by the end of week two there will be shop-floor meetings at over two hundred plants, and it is estimated that we can bring out almost a million workers on two-day protest strikes. There will be demonstrations in Trafalgar Square against Canada House and against the US Embassy in Grosvenor Square. We have a special squad to harass the American Ambassador wherever he goes, and at that stage there will be similar protests in all the other NATO countries. Then—"

Gouzenko interrupted. "You mentioned last week an analysis of protesters done by Z-Eleven Research. Can you give us some details?"

Yessov sighed but knew better than to refuse and pulled out a plastic cover and leafed through the papers.

"The Z-Eleven analysis is based on research and a survey of public opinion carried out when the British joined the Common Market. Over ninety percent of the objectors were objecting on grounds of 'losing national independence.' It started as a typical protest by retired colonels and country ladies but in the end it covered all social groups, and the common factor was the old dislike of foreigners. There's a similar survey about British public attitudes to immigrants—it's not only blacks they don't like, it's pretty well everyone. There's a report by Goebbels' Propaganda Ministry in 1943 showing a violent dislike, by British men and troops, of American servicemen. Goebbels' ministry played on it very heavily right to the end of the war."

Levin was half smiling. "What makes this operation so right is that all our information over the last six months indicates that the Americans would be delighted to move their troops out of NATO anyway."

Gouzenko interrupted again. "They won't want to give up their investments in Britain, though."

Yessov nodded. "True, but it makes no odds to this operation. This whole operation only has one objective: to create a situation that is likely to lead to the Americans pulling out of NATO—or being thrown out. Nothing else matters. The industrial unrest in Britain, the friction between the governments—it's a plus but it's a side issue. The Yanks want out, they're sick of playing policeman for the rest of the world, they don't want to pay their share of NATO, and all we are doing is giving them the excuse they've been looking for."

"You think they won't analyze the setup and hang on just to keep the balance?" Levin asked.

Gouzenko leaned back. "My dear Levin, there *isn't* a balance, even *with* the Americans in NATO." He pulled a card from his pocket and scanned it quickly before saying, "As of yesterday the Warsaw powers have

133

at least a three-to-one superiority to NATO in every function—troops, weapons, aircraft and ships—except nuclear submarines, and it's been like that since the summer of '72. NATO is a waste of time and money and every NATO government knows it, and after this operation the people will know it too."

Yessov leaned forward. "They'll rise up when they know the facts and—"

Gouzenko was smiling. "They won't rise up, comrade, they're too interested in color TV sets, new cars and freezers, and all the rest of it. Our operation wouldn't work if it was based on revelations about NATO. Rudenko will make it work because they envy and hate the Americans and we're giving them a good, rational, honest excuse to do it out loud."

Yessov waited to see if the other two had any other comments. "Do you agree we ought to do an appreciation of the situation after Snowball?" He glanced from the corner of his eye at Gouzenko, who waited to see if Levin would speak. When he didn't, Gouzenko looked up at Yessov's face and tapped his thick finger on the table as he spoke.

"Comrade Yessov, I strongly recommend you to confine your thinking to Operation Snowball. It's only in phase one as yet, and when it's over you can rest assured the High Command will give you adequate instructions." He looked aside at Levin. "Don't be misled by Comrade Yessov, my friend. Somewhere in his fine office there'll be a nice little plastic file elegantly examining the troop reductions possible when Snowball is over." He stood up and puffed out his cheeks, and the little piggy eyes were smiling. "You'd better add another paragraph to your appreciation, Comrade Yessov. What reductions can we make in the KGB budget when we're controlling Europe? You just think about that." And he tapped Yessov's chest with the back of a very hard hand. He glanced from one to another. "You reckon that Rudenko can do this?"

Yessov looked at his drink and swirled it gently around the deep glass. Then, looking up, he said, "He's a first-class operator, he's got all the resources he's asked for, and we've activated all the suitable contacts of two apparats, so there's no reason for failure."

Levin said, "Do we agree that Rudenko starts phase two now?"

Gouzenko walked over to his belt and coat, and as he was putting them on he said, "Agreed."

He saluted them both and left them.

The battalion commander and Major Bross from Defense HQ were waiting in the big, cold hall, and they stood to attention for a full five minutes and got an earful of acid about laziness and inefficiency. The unit was due for three weeks' leave when their Lubyanka duty was over in two days' time. Gouzenko canceled the leave and arranged for a month of recruit training for one and all.

As Gouzenko stamped down the steps he glanced at the guards and saw that they were now carrying carbines. He turned up his coat collar and stepped out briskly, stamping his feet and swinging his arms. At Manege Square he caught sight of one of the Kremlin spires. There was a meeting of the Praesidium Planning Committee during the next few days, and he wondered what they would do if he walked in and told them not to plan beyond the next two months because their days were numbered.

The building he approached wasn't the usual Moscow gray; it was shining white and faintly oriental. The Military Museum had been closed for two hours. There were no cars outside, but he knew that a bomb on the museum in the next hour could wipe out all that mattered of the armed forces' High Command. Ever since he'd done it he'd worried about having pulled the card with the NATO details from his tunic pocket. Fortunately Yessov was too full of his own importance to notice; he spent his time trying to dominate everybody and was not very observant. Apart from that, he'd probably think that every full colonel had such details. Or maybe, that he had those facts as part of his liaison function. It had been a slip, but he'd bet his next leave that neither of them had noticed anything.

The main door lock had been changed eight months ago and the new key was a thick rod of about 16 mm diameter, made out of steel and machined to a very fine tolerance that tapered from its full diameter to a sharp point in a series of cylindrical steps. He thrust it into the orifice and it turned easily and smoothly. A set of four plug tumblers lifted one after the other and the door opened. The glass cases that stood in long rows housed regimental relics and documents, but he could only just make out their shapes because the lights were very dim in the big, spacious hall. His boots echoed on the polished parquet floor, and when he was approaching the doors at the far end he saw the glow of a cigarette. A few more steps and he made out the handsome, saturnine face of Marshal Rokossovsky, hero of the Don but thrown out by the Poles after he'd been awarded to them as their Minister of Defense. They'd weighed him up and despite his name they counted him as Russian to the soles of his military boots. Full of Polish charm maybe, a magnificent tactician and fighter, but Russian all the way through.

Rokossovsky put his hand on Gouzenko's arm and leaned forward to open the door. He waved Gouzenko through. "They're waiting for you."

There were nine men in uniform. The only navy man was an admiral; the rest were mere colonels and most of them were gray-haired. They were sitting around a long table and there were only three lights in the room. The lights had green shades and were low slung so that above them the ceiling was lost in darkness, and below, the men's faces had the appearance of portraits in oils, because the lighting was harsh and flat.

Rokossovsky stood leaning forward over the back of his chair at the head of the table. All eyes were on his face and he needed no artifice to get their attention; they were waiting for him to speak. "I want to remind you, my friends, that we are here tonight to consider the mobile bridge units and their malfunction in Operation Dnieper."

He paused for a few moments and the faces were impassive. They knew what they were here for and they knew the cover story only too well. But Rokossovsky waited until finally a man at the far end of the table said, "We take your point, Konstantin, we take your point."

Rokossovsky waited for a moment, then walked around his chair and sat down. He leaned back and turned to a younger man halfway down the table on his right. "Lev, have you anything to report?"

The man shrugged like a Frenchman. "No, Marshal, there was some problem of tank routing near Bruges—there are canal repairs—but we understand they should be finished by tomorrow." He looked with big brown eyes at Rokossovsky. "My group still awaits final instructions in the Adriatic. Do we go beyond Trieste if there is no opposition?"

Rokossovsky raised his eyebrows and looked heavenward. "My dear Lev, an order not given is an order itself. The plan is the plan—we stop at Trieste." Rokossovsky didn't even look to his right to observe the man's reaction to the reproof; he just turned to Gouzenko. "Well now, Nikita, what is your news?"

Gouzenko looked around at the others before speaking. Then, marking the points off on his thick fingers, he said, "Point one—Operation Snowball goes to phase two tonight, a KGB responsibility. Point two—phase one has been fully implemented, in my view successfully. Point three—they have no idea in either the KGB or the GRU of what Snowball is really about."

Rokossovsky nodded his acknowledgment, and looking down at the table as if collecting his thoughts, he said, "Well, gentlemen, this is it. We represent phase four of Snowball, the physical occupation of Europe from the Baltic to the Adriatic. I think none of us has any doubt about phase four. We have spent two years on it, from feasibility study to operational orders. It will be over by the seventh day at the worst and the third day at best. It doesn't matter which it is to us, but" —and his head was turned aside like a thrush listening on a lawn and he wagged a finger in emphasis—"but we have to decide tonight exactly what success we require from phase three of Snowball before we start phase four." He leaned back and waited.

A colonel with tank insignia sitting a few places from Gouzenko caught Rokossovsky's eye and started speaking. "General, we need nothing from this political plan. We can do what is required of us tomorrow if you give the order."

Rokossovsky looked around the table to see if anyone intended replying, but nobody spoke; they were all looking at him. "It is nearly seven months since we finalized our plans, and it is easy for a man to forget everything except what he himself is responsible for. My friend here is correct, we can occupy Europe in four bloody days, but using the phases of Snowball we do several positive things. When I said four bloody days I remind myself that some of that blood will be ours. The more that local populations see the Americans as self-seeking and disloyal the easier our operation will be, and"—he was nodding his head to emphasize each word —"our task in organizing the occupation will be that much easier afterward. Guerrillas we shall have, but if they know the Americans were ready to make a deal with the Nazis they will draw their own conclusions. I am also advised—and I agree—that it will help calm the American people's reactions if they are already disenchanted with the Europeans. It has all been analyzed precisely and I'm told it is important that there be maximum popular unrest, particularly in Great Britain."

He paused and then continued with a slight smile.

"Remember, too, that if it is not successful in its first phases it provides one more reason for dealing with the KGB. We must not forget that they want to show the Soviets that they can conquer Europe without the Armed Forces of the Union. The Party tigers went along with their thinking, and if it had worked, my friends, make no mistake—they had plans for us." The thick hairy fingers of both hands were splayed out with his pressure on the tabletop. "You have my assurance that every unit of the Soviet armed forces is as one with us; otherwise we should not be here. Let us continue as we have planned. We have nothing to lose. If the first three phases succeed even partially, we shall have saved resources and lives." His eyes were afire with zeal, as his hand smacked the table in time with his final words. "All we are doing, my friends, is collecting the prize we paid for, that the politicians threw away in 1945."

A quick glance around the table and he saw the nodding heads and heard the muttered agreement. His voice went on, this time quiet and even.

"Now let us return to our examination." He pointed down the table. "Gregor, I understand General Susloparov is raising the problem of food supplies and distribution in Sicily and in the Schleswig-Holstein islands.

Fourth Army staff *and* third-year officer students at the Academy have both done recent appreciations of this problem. Also there are revised lists for Paris and Brussels of minimum destruction buildings that will be required for army headquarters. The decision has also been taken that offshore islands, including the Channel Islands, will not be occupied. There will also be copies available down to Division Headquarters of the collaborators' address manuals. They are top secret and—"

They talked and argued until the early hours of the next morning and left either singly or in pairs. As Gouzenko left he looked up at the low, fast-moving clouds and hoped he would be attached to 9th and 14th Armies, who were going to settle some old scores in West Germany.

19

THERE WAS A SUDDEN SWIRL of snow as Yessov leaned against the alcove and looked out of the window. It had come early this year. There probably wouldn't be many more weekends at the dacha at Penickov. Winter in the countryside was all right for families but not for well-off bachelors. It was four days since the meeting with Gouzenko about Operation Snowball. There was something Gouzenko had said or had done that stayed on the edge of his mind like a wolf on the edge of a forest. He shook his head in irritation and dismissal. It was probably nothing of importance, and it would come back to him if he stopped thinking about it. Maybe it was something he was going to ask Gouzenko that had slipped his mind.

He walked quickly across to his desk and locked the drawers and the filing cabinets. It was nearly twenty minutes later when he had cleared the final security net, and as he walked down the steps the wind cut into his face but there was no more snow. He'd arranged for a car from the KGB pool at the Kremlin guard center and he stepped out briskly.

There was a Red Army helicopter drifting in a constant figure-eight about three hundred feet above the familiar onion-topped towers, and even as he looked it swung and tilted and the sun blazed in an orange flame on the cockpit windows as it eased off to the helicopter patrol base at Kuntsevo. The sun caught the onion tops, and the gold crenellations sparkled and shone, and the Kremlin complex suddenly looked like a Bolshoi set for *Aida*. It made him think of a poem his mother had been fond of about the golden domes of Samarkand. He'd always meant to go to Samarkand, it had sounded so romantic when he was young, but now it was just the headquarters of Uzbekistan Subarea of the KGB—a place to avoid.

He signed for the car, and after collecting his bags from his flat he headed eastward to the main beltway and then across the main road onto the road to Orekhovo. It was dark now and the car's headlights left behind the men and women cycling home to their villages, and soon even the long buses grew scarce and it was only the massed conifers of the woods that were picked out by the lights.

When Snowball was completed he understood that he would be posted to Paris with a promotion and all the trimmings. He knew Paris well and he would be able to pick up old contacts—as well as make new ones. After all, some of the girls would be almost thirty now, probably married with kids. Over the fields to his right he could see the evening express to Kisov, long lines of lighted windows. It stayed with him for almost ten miles and then swung away and was lost in the darkness.

All through the summer Yessov had spent most of his weekends at the dacha. It was a frame structure with a large lounge and a pleasant bedroom. There was a magnificent bathroom with a beautiful old-fashioned bath in decorated porcelain. An old *babcha* from the village cleaned up and looked after the place when he was away. There was a big garden where the old lady's husband was allowed to grow fruit and vegetables. The dacha was on the edge of a small town which was itself a couple of miles from Orekhovo.

142

The lights were on in the house when he turned the car up the rough dirt path, and when he had switched off the car engine he stood for a few moments in the darkness. The sky was overcast and the clouds raced past the moon, but the wind was high and only lightly moved the tops of the pines that circled the house. A frog croaked, and as his eyes grew accustomed to the dark, Yessov saw the house lights shining across the tall heads of chrysanthemums in the garden near the windows. Then the pathway was lit with golden light from the open door, and the old lady came out to help him with his bags. Ten minutes later she had left and he was on his own.

He'd told her to knock on the girl's window, and while he waited he ate some ham and salad that the *babcha* had left for him. She had lit the stove and the room was warm and smelled pleasantly of burning applewood. Yessov enjoyed these country weekends with his books and without the pressures of Moscow and work. The girl suited the place and the tempo. A few months after he had been allocated the dacha she had come to the door to sell fresh eggs and had stayed with him all that night. That was just over a year ago and she had been only seventeen. She had none of the sexual prowess of the Moscow girls who shared his bed from time to time, but she was far prettier and completely and innocently complaisant. Whatever he wanted to do to her she allowed, not grudgingly but casually and easily like a beautiful young animal. He gave her money from time to time and small trinkets from Moscow, which seemed to please her more. It was an easy, relaxed relationship and she never came unless he sent for her. Over the last months of summer she had stayed with him each weekend until he left for Moscow early on Monday morning. She liked to talk to him about the people in Moscow and the girls in the Bolshoi, and when he wanted to read she would lie relaxed like a cat on the big low bed, naked and natural with eyes half closed and her breathing the rhythm of sleep and love. He looked over now at the bed. On top of the fox fur coverlet was the present from Moscow—a pale straw hat with cornflowers and poppies at the brim—and he smiled at the thought of her pleasure and in his mind's eye saw her standing, smiling and naked except for the straw hat.

Half an hour later she arrived, and as she sat on the bed trying on the hat he looked over at her. She looked almost Swedish with the long blond hair and the bright blue eyes, and as she held up her arms to arrange the straw hat he saw the big full breasts and he couldn't wait to have her. The girl had seen his eyes and she laughed at him and stood up with the hat perched on her head and said teasingly, "You want to see me with just my new hat." He didn't answer but she knew what he wanted, and a few seconds later she stood facing him, long legs apart and the big firm breasts naked and heavy. One hand was lifted up to hold the straw hat, and the other hung loosely behind her. There was no mistaking the message—she was available, and as he pulled her over to him she laughed and tossed the hat on the bed and made no attempt to hide her willingness as his body moved against her.

Almost two hours later Yessov lay back with his head on the pillows and the girl lay with her full breasts cradled in his groin. She was eating an apple as they talked, and as she moved on her elbows she smiled at Yessov and he said, "Keep still, girl, you're leading me on."

She laughed. "Let's talk of graveyards and then you'll go down again."

He grinned. "Let's talk about you instead. How's the dashing lieutenant of artillery these days?"

The lieutenant commanded a battery that was stationed in the village. He was twenty-eight and handsome and he wanted her to marry him. He had courted the girl for a year and knew nothing of Yessov and their relationship. The courtship was formal and very proper, and from time to time the girl had talked about him to Yessov, who smiled faintly and was not impressed. He never said anything unkind about the young lieutenant; his jokes were gentle even though they were disparaging. He had no reason to be jealous, he had the girl as often as he wanted her, there was nothing she wouldn't let him do, and the lieutenant got nothing but chaste kisses and not many of those.

The girl pouted and said, "He's a very nice boy. I think we'll be getting married very soon."

Yessov leaned up and pulled her so that she was on top of him and her mouth was on his. He murmured, "You'll make him a wonderful wife," but she knew from experience what she had to do. And as she knelt astride him she kissed him passionately as he enjoyed her. He was still in her when he said casually, "Why do you think you'll marry him sooner?"

She leaned back, not entirely unaware of his eyes on her young body, and stroking his leg she said, "He'll be moving soon, and then if things go well he'll be made captain and he can get permission to marry."

"I thought artillery men had to wait for permanent quarters—don't move about like that."

The girl said eagerly, "Well, he will be permanent after this move if all goes well."

"Where's he moving to?"

"To Hannover."

"When does he go there?"

"We don't know exactly, but the unit is on full alert so it won't be long."

He leaned up, frowning. "What do you mean about the unit? You mean they're all going? It's impossible."

"It isn't impossible, because he knows. They've had special orders."

"But Hannover's in West Germany. We don't have Red Army units there—you've got it wrong."

The girl flushed and said, "That's what he told me, and all the officers have been learning German every night."

She leaned back and looked down at his face and smiled a superior smile as she saw him looking up at her breasts; even at eighteen she knew that those gave her the last word. He smiled up at her. "Show me," he said, and she knelt up so that he could see her and the conversation ended.

It was well past midnight when they were eating, and as they ate he listened to a radio performance of Rachmaninov's *Isle of the Dead*. But something buzzed and bumbled like an irritated fly in Yessov's mind, something the girl had said that didn't make sense. His hand was in a bowl of raisins when it all clicked together.

"Did you say that the artillery unit is on full alert?"

She nodded her head without looking up, as she picked over some almost green tomatoes. "Yes, that's what he said."

"And you said the move would be permanent if all goes well?"

She nodded.

"If what goes well?"

She shrugged. "If—whatever soldiers do goes well —the battle or whatever."

He put a towel around his waist and moved over to the phone. Even out there it had a scrambler, but he didn't use it for the first call to the KGB Order of Battle section. It seemed the artillery unit in the village was B Battery of 17 Squadron attached for all duties to the Rostov Assault Division. And the password for the day was Dynamo. For the second call he used the scrambler button; and when he'd given the password he asked for Operations Control. The girl had come across to stand by him as he leaned carelessly against the wall. When the voice spoke up at the other end he said, "Give me next week's operational orders for B Battery of Seventeen Squadron, attached to the Rostov Assault Division. Password Dynamo."

"A moment, comrade."

He whistled softly as he waited, and the girl sensed that he was no longer relaxed. Then he was alert as he listened to the phone. "B Battery has routine orders for next week, comrade."

"And the next week?"

"Just a moment."

He sensed that he was on to something despite all the negative responses. He smiled at the girl, and as he turned back to the phone she slid her hand under the towel.

There was a different voice on the other end of the phone, sharper and authoritative. "Are you inquiring about a unit in Rostov Assault?"

"Yes, comrade."

"What is the basis of your inquiry?"

Yessov's voice hardened. "No basis, comrade, just password Dynamo, and may I remind you that under Section Eight it is forbidden to probe inquiry sources if the correct password is given. Do you query Dynamo?"

"No, comrade. I assume you are KGB liaison so I must ask you to wait while I check. This unit is not on the printout."

"Why not, comrade?"

"No details, comrade, but I'll check."

Yessov didn't answer but put his hand over the mouthpiece and smiled at the girl. "Young Nadia, you may be right after all about your lieutenant."

The girl's hand gently caressed him but he didn't

respond, not even when she took his hand and closed it over her right breast.

Then he turned his head quickly because there was yet another voice on the phone, relaxed but rough. "Good day, comrade, can I help you?"

"Yes, comrade, just answer my simple question."

"This is comrade General Marov. The information is likely to take an hour to check—it seems this unit is not on the main computer and we shall have to check with second-echelon records. Is it all that important?"

"No, comrade, not at all. Shall I call you again tomorrow?"

"Excellent, comrade, let's do that."

Yessov hung up the phone gently and was barely aware of the girl. There was something going on, all right, with generals answering routine queries and giving phony excuses for not giving the information. The possibility of an assault division like the Rostov not being on the operations computer was too remote to need a second thought. He looked at the girl and was conscious that his body had reacted to her hand. She was so young and so pretty and he had planned to have her for two whole days, but today was only Saturday and only two hours old and she'd have to go. He pulled her to him, his hands holding her firm round buttocks. "Nadia, I'll take you back. I've got to work." He made no move to let her go, and she could feel his excitement.

She smiled gently. "Do you want me again before I go?"

He stroked her soft cheek and looked in the blue eyes. "Can you tell?"

She nodded. "Of course."

He sighed, and it was not pretense. "It doesn't seem decent to do it like that—in a hurry."

She pushed gently against him. "I don't mind if it's what you want." Hurry or no hurry, it was nearly an hour before they were dressed and getting into the car. The straw hat was on the back seat and Yessov was touched for a moment by its importance to the girl, but it wasn't enough to slow down the effect of the adrenalin in his veins. He knew he had found something that a general wanted to hide. It was corruption or treason. Generals don't cover up for less.

20

WHEN YESSOV GOT BACK to the dacha he put more coal on the tiled stove and sat at the small table. He took out his pen and started writing a list of names and telephone numbers on a message pad from his leather briefcase. Then he pulled the phone across to the table and started down the list. At the end of an hour he had checked various items of information with four departments of the State and the Secretariat of the Praesidium. Nothing he had said, or asked for, had aroused any curiosity or suspicion for he had worded his requests very carefully.

What he had learned didn't make sense—unless there was something terribly wrong somewhere. And if what he feared was wrong was true, he had to find out right away and decide what to do. There were twenty-four assault divisions not on the central computer. They had been taken off a week ago. This should mean that they were undergoing training or regrouping. The five that had been checked on had all clammed up at top level, and this in itself was suspicious, as routine inquiries would have normally been dealt with by divisional liaison staff. Divisional commanders wouldn't waste their time on such matters—unless it was to scare off the inquirer. And why were they off the central control computer, which recorded every signal and order? There was no military exercise planned; they had not long stood down from Exercise Dnieper. He could phone Gouzenko as the official liaison link between the Red

Army and the KGB, but some instinct told him to avoid this. But he had checked on Gouzenko's whereabouts and found that he was in East Berlin, and that too seemed odd.

He knew that checking on the girl's story at the artillery unit would be the most fruitful action, but something held him back from doing this. It was like touching a pair of copper wires that might be live; there was an impulse to do it but experience said do some more checking before taking this step. He went down his list and there was no more checking he could do. He walked to the window and looked across the garden. The sky was gray and the poor light made the trees at the edge of the wood look black and ominous. He shivered and without thinking walked over to his briefcase and rummaged through till he found the pistol.

The artillery unit was based at a derelict wooden mill which now carried a sign saying B Battery HQ. He stood by the car for a moment and looked around. There were guns draped with the latest camouflage nets and each one was guarded by men with rifles. He noticed they had fixed bayonets and wondered if that was normal. As he looked a tall slim lieutenant marched toward him. He was hatless and his fair hair lifted in the gusty wind. He had very blue eyes and freckles, and Yessov could see that many village girls would find him a very desirable catch. Before the young man could speak, Yessov showed him his identity card. The blue eyes checked his face against the photograph and read carefully through the description and then handed it back.

"How can I help you, comrade Yessov?"

"Shall we go in your office and talk, comrade lieutenant?"

The young man led the way and told a clerk to leave them alone. There were maps on the walls, and orders in steel clips hung on nails. A photograph of Lenin and a colored poster of Brezhnev and a marshal of the Red

Army in all his glory. He looked closer and saw that it was the old Polish warhorse, Rokossovsky. The Lieutenant showed him to a chair at the trestle table and sat down himself on the other side.

Yessov leaned back and studied the lieutenant's face without speaking. The blue eyes held his look and were not abashed. Yessov guessed that whatever was going on in this unit was being done under orders from Divisional HQ. Matching the other's face carefully, Yessov said, "*Sprechen Sie ganz gutes Deutsch?*"

The young man smiled and shrugged. "*Leider bin Ich kein Fachman der Deutsche Sprache—trotzdem bin Ich. . . .*" Then he stopped and said in Russian, "Why are we speaking German, comrade?"

Yessov looked at him but said nothing for a minute or so. "I have had reports that members of your unit have ignored security regulations."

"In what respect, comrade?"

Yessov leaned back and watched the young man's eyes intently. "They've talked about Hannover, lieutenant."

It worked; the blue eyes had flickered and there was a flush mounting the lieutenant's cheeks. He stood up and walked across to the stove. When he swung around to face Yessov, he said, "If you'll give me the names and details I'll see that they are duly punished."

Yessov smiled. "I'm afraid it's not so easy as that, comrade."

"Oh? Why not?"

"When did you get your orders about Hannover, comrade?"

"The last day of September."

"Written or verbal?"

"The exercise was in writing. The orders were by telephone."

"Where from?"

"Moscow HQ."

152

"Who gave them?"

"A General Gouzenko."

"Did you note the time and the actual words?"

"Yes."

"Let me see your notes."

"I made only a mental note."

Yessov looked at the lieutenant and there was no smile now. "Comrade, you know the punishment for discussing any operational matters with civilians."

The young man was trembling visibly. "Yes, comrade—I know. What am I to do?"

He looked as though he might faint, and Yessov waved him back to the chair.

"Tell me, lieutenant, what were the verbal orders?"

The man closed his eyes in concentration and then said slowly, " 'Exercise now an operation as from twenty-four hundred hours thirtieth October.' "

"The exercise was covered by written orders?"

"Yes, comrade."

"Let me see them."

The face was haggard and drawn and the hand that helped him to stand hung loosely as the lieutenant moved to the small standard army safe. He unlocked it with two keys and there was a thin file on top of the other papers and the lieutenant's hand shook as he handed it across to Yessov. There was a printed contents page headed with the legend Operation Snowball. Then there were twelve closely typed pages of narrative and detailed orders. Although he realized something was terribly wrong, Yessov was too confused with disbelief to take in all the implications. Finally he told the young officer to close the safe, and when that was done he said very quietly, "Comrade lieutenant. I am taking charge of these documents, and I suggest you don't discuss my visit with anybody—do you understand?"

21

YESSOV WAS BACK in Moscow by noon that day, and on
the journey he'd sorted out a rough plan of action. He
didn't check in his official car but parked it near the
Moscow University buildings. As he walked across Red
Square there was a pale sunshine lighting the long queue
at the Mausoleum and a press photographer was taking a
picture of one of the guards talking to a girl with a
bouquet of white daisies. It was a typical Moscow Saturday and the people looked relaxed, with time to waste.
He noticed that the police had allowed the flower sellers
to come back again with their buckets and barrows, and
it reminded him of a picture that had hung on the wall
at home when he was a boy. It was this same square with
the flower sellers and the crowds but their clothes were of
the last century. The picture's title was on a small gold-
painted plaque on the ornate gilded frame, and it said
"Red Square Moscow 1875"—it was called Red Square
even then because, in that old Russian, red and beautiful
were the same word. He noticed the helicopter was
back again, and this time it hung steady for a few minutes about a quarter of a mile away. Yessov half smiled
as he guessed the pilot was probably breaking orders by
hanging over the stadium where Moscow Dynamo was
playing a friendly game against Ajax of Amsterdam. He
passed two militiamen talking together as they strolled,
and Yessov saw one of them look at him as if he were

suspicious. It was nonsense, he knew, but it was part of his tension. When he'd made the plan for the flight of the English defectors Burgess and Maclean he had had only thirty-six hours, but he had arranged everything without hesitation or doubt in less than five hours from getting his orders. They were out a full day ahead and already in Moscow before they were missed. If the results of his investigations in the next two hours were positive, he would be planning his own escape by the time the football crowds were on their way home. And he couldn't even decide where to go. London and New York were obvious but quite the most difficult. Paris, Stockholm, or Helsinki would be much easier. Berlin was out; he wouldn't stand a cat in hell's chance that way. He wasn't even aware of the guards as he went up the steps at the Lubyanka.

Half an hour later he already knew enough. He had telephoned to the KGB liaison officers of ten of the twenty-four divisions which had been taken off the control computer. Not one was available. Sick leave, compassionate leave, refresher courses, weapons courses, annual leave, cross-postings to other units, weekend leave—every official excuse or reason that any army has ever devised apart from death or defection was proferred as grounds that kept him from speaking to the KGB man on the spot. In no case had he pressed the point. All had been sweet reason and light. The excuses were so wide-ranging that he concluded even those had been properly fixed to avoid suspicious repetition.

He had walked down the long corridor to the transport and travel section and checked various routes and timetables at the reference shelves, and then there had been a messenger. Would he report to the duty officer? The duty officer had received a signal from Signals Security section marked "To be read by most senior officer." He held the buff envelope and tapped it on his other hand as he spoke to his colleague. "You've checked that I am the most senior officer here at the moment?"

"Yes, sir. Comrade Laski will be here at four, but a Security Signals message has to be processed immediately."

Yessov nodded and casually opened the envelope and read the message. He looked over at the junior and said, "I'll go and deal with it. Put it in the register at thirteen seventeen hours, number ten twenty-three—today's date."

The junior said, "Right, comrade. You'll let me have the original in due course?"

"Of course. Give it description as follows: Routine intercept notification."

"Thank you, comrade."

Yessov deliberately walked slowly back to his office. He'd been wanting a sign, something to push him one way or another. This was it.

He sat down at his desk and read it again. It said:

MESSAGE KGB 19771023 EX SIGNALS SECURITY TO MOST SENIOR OFFICER LUBYANKA SECRETARIAT STOP RADIO TRAFFIC TODAY EX B BATTERY—17 SQUADRON— ROSTOV ASSAULT INDICATES COMMANDER CONTACTED 3RD ARMY REPEAT 3RD ARMY DIRECT STOP INDICATED VISIT BY POSSIBLE KGB OFFICER UNNAMED STOP INDICATED CONSIDERABLE CONCERN 3RD ARMY HQ STOP KGB DE-SCRIPTION REQUESTED STOP 3RD ARMY HAS CONTACTED 5TH AND 19TH REPEAT 5TH AND 19TH ARMIES ON SUBJECT STOP NO KGB UNIT CONTACTED BY THEM ON RADIO STOP REQUEST YOU CHECK IF OTHER CONTACT TO KGB STOP WORD SNOWBALL USED FOUR TIMES POSSI-BLY CODEWORD NOT ON OUR LIST INTERNAL STOP CON-TINUING MONITORING BUT EXPECT SUBJECTS WILL TRANS-FER TELEPHONE OR MULTILINK VHF STOP REQUEST

So the young lieutenant really had got the wind up, enough to risk his indiscretions being punished severely, and for some reason he'd gone direct to the higher level, short-circuiting his squadron HQ, division HQ, and corps HQ. There was no doubt now that the Red Army had surreptitiously taken over Operation Snowball and was turning it into a military operation. And if they had cut out the KGB it meant that they'd cut out the Party as well, and that meant that when the Praesidium was informed there was going to be a very big bang. The Red Army would probably come out on top eventually, but the whole fabric of control would be destroyed and it would take decades to build it up again. Everything still depended on Snowball moving on through its final phases as originally planned. If he reported what he had discovered to either side he'd probably be given the Order of Lenin—posthumously.

He folded up the signal and put it in his inside pocket. He stood up, took a bunch of keys from his pocket, and walked over to the small wall safe. From there he took his passport, his special KGB pass for use overseas, and a book of travel warrants. When he had closed the safe he stamped each of the travel warrants with the Central Secretariat authority and pressed the bell on his desk. When the orderly came he told him to find Suchov. While he waited he considered withdrawing his own savings from the bank and then decided against it. If anything went wrong it would show that he had seen his mission as entirely official if he only used official funds. Anyway, if it came to it he could always make a financial deal with the Americans or the British or even the French. When Suchov knocked and entered, Yessov told him he wanted $10,000 US

157

in cash. The money, in two separate envelopes, was with him ten minutes later. He signed the chit and then as Suchov closed the door Yessov wrote on two pieces of notepaper just the date and the words Operation Snowball. He folded them, put them in two envelopes, and addressed one to "Colonel Gouzenko, Red Army/KGB liaison," the other to "Colonel Levin, GRU/KGB liaison." He put both envelopes in the top right-hand drawer of his desk.

The giant TU-104 jet airliner had sixty comfortable armchairs, brown and gold wallpaper, lace curtains, china figurines in glass cases, and heavy mahogany tables. Yessov was getting VIP treatment, and it seemed no time at all before they were rolling to a noisy halt on the main runway at East Berlin's Gatow airport. It was early evening but the airport buildings were busy and crowded. Yessov bought a razor and a few toiletries, and with a couple of paperbacks these made a small, neat parcel. Two men were watching him from a balcony on the next floor up, and as he went through one of the main doors they nodded to a man standing near the bookstall. There were several queues for taxis, but Yessov was in no hurry. It was nearly ten minutes later when he walked up to the only taxi left and with one hand on the door he nodded to the driver. "*Vier Jahreszeiten, bitte.*" The man nodded and Yessov opened the door with his free hand.

It was only then that he saw the man with the gun. The man patted the seat beside him and smiling said, "Come along, friend—take a seat." Yessov made to back out of the car but there were two men there right behind him. The man was still smiling but the muzzle of the gun didn't waver. Yessov reluctantly got in and the man spoke in German to the driver and the car moved off into the traffic.

The man slid the gun into the pocket of his coat

158

and turned to Yessov. His eyes were almost yellow, and together with the aquiline nose he reminded Yessov of a vulture he'd seen in the Moscow zoo. Yessov said in poor German, "Who are you and what the devil do you think you are doing?"

The man looked back at him reflectively and calmly and said nothing. The shops and office blocks gradually gave way to old-fashioned suburban streets and then even larger detached houses standing in their own grounds. Yessov saw a sign which said Jacobi Strasse, and as the car came to a stop the driver got out and opened two big wrought-iron gates and then got back in the car. There was a curved drive of red asphalt and a well-cut lawn setting off a large old-fashioned house. The other man got out and Yessov saw that the gun was in his hand again. This time the man spoke in Russian. "Get out, Yessov, and walk slowly toward the green door." When he got out of the car the air was warm and there was a pleasant fresh smell of newly cut grass. Against the front wall were espaliered pears hung with their heavy crop, and butterflies settled with spread wings on the Michaelmas daisies. He was conscious of the warmth and light compared with Moscow, and there was an air of quiet peace that reminded him of when he was a boy. Even the man with the gun was calm and half smiling.

Inside, the house was neat and clean. There was a hum of voices and a clatter of dishes from the back of the house. The gun waved him to the broad stairs and they ended in a room that had one wall lined with books, four armchairs, and some plain Swedish office furniture. The man with the gun handed it over to the car driver and left the room. The driver waved Yessov to one of the armchairs.

The man had walked downstairs and was now locked in a small room on the ground floor. There were red quarry tiles on the floor, and he knelt down and slid a thin blade between two tiles under a small mahogany table. Then with a sideways movement of the knife four tiles lifted away and the man eased out a metal-clad radio. He plugged in a thin cord that hung in the folds of a curtain, and a neon display lit up a panel of small dials. The man moved without hurrying and pulled up a chair to where the radio equipment lay on the small table. He slowly turned a dial and the neon display started flashing in short bursts. Then he turned a second dial and the light slowed down till it blinked so slowly it was like drops of water from a dripping tap. Then the man flicked the switch and there was the solid hiss of a carrier wave and almost at once a voice was clearly saying "Thirty-thirty-thirty-thirty." The man opened a small leather case and took out a small gelatin square marked "thirty" and slid it into the guide slots on the front of the radio. He pressed the button below and the sine-wave display on the oscilloscope slowly closed in on the sine wave on the gelatin. The voice was still repeating "Thirty-thirty-thirty" slowly and distinctly. Then the two sine waves coincided and the voice cut out. A small red light pulsed and the man started speaking.

"Your scrambler not indicating, repeat, not indicating," and as he spoke a second red light started pulsing.

"Control here, control here, what is current state of game?"

"We picked him up at the airport as instructed."

"Have you carried out initial interrogation yet?"

"No, we have only just arrived at base, but I don't foresee any difficulties."

"Why not?"

"I don't know, just instinct, I suppose. Has Anders been informed?"

"Yes, he's here. Do you want to talk to him?"

"Yes."

Anders linked in. "How are you, Ed?"

"Fine, Tad. We've got the KGB man and we expect the written details of this Snowball job in the next half hour. What do you want to know, anything special?"

"The lot, Ed, everything you can get. Just go over how you got onto this guy. They've told me what you've said before but I'd like to hear it from you."

"Late this afternoon I got a tip-off. Must have been at least at second or third hand. The girl didn't know much but she gave us the name Yessov and said he was KGB and then gave us the flight number and said, 'Tell Yessov the snowball's melting.' That was it. She wouldn't say any more. I don't think she knew any more."

"Any idea of who was using her to contact you?"

"Oh, could be KGB or GRU. She's one of the better-class tarts who hang around the KGB resthouse in Leine Strasse. But I had her tagged after she left me, and although she dodged around a bit she went back to a Red Army HQ in Pankow and reported to a Colonel Gouzenko. You can probably check him at your end. There's nothing on our files, but West Berlin may have him."

"What do you think it's all about?"

"Well, I gather that this snowball jazz has some significance your end."

"True. It's a KGB operation, high grade and current."

"Well, it could be the army or the GRU putting a spoke in the operation or just in Yessov."

"You remember the man with code name Butler?"

"Sure, the KGB guy who helped transit Burgess and Maclean."

"That's him. He didn't help, he did it. That's Yessov."

"Is that what you want me to concentrate on?"

"No, Ed, that's background. Operation Snowball is what matters. I want all you can get but particularly timing. If you think it's worth it I'll come over, but I'm pretty hard pressed here. I suggest you do no more than two hours before you report back, and then hourly."

"OK, Tad. Roger easy."

"Roger."

Back in the upstairs room the man nodded to the driver and held out his hand for the gun. The driver left, closing the door quietly behind him. The man looked across at Yessov. He reminded him of someone but he couldn't remember who. It was a thin, handsome face. The alert mind, the observant eyes were obvious. "Well, comrade Yessov, have you worked it all out yet?"

Yessov leaned back and moved one shoulder nervously as he smiled. His fingers were laced together to cover up his tension. "I think so. You must be SIS. From what I recall from the files you must be Ed Farrow. You came here last December. If I may say so you look younger than your age—at least the age on our file."

Farrow was rolling a pencil along the flat arm of the chair, seemingly absorbed in this civil engineering. Without looking up he said quietly, "How do you think we ought to deal with this, Yessov?" and then he did look up and watched Yessov's face.

Yessov pursed his lips and said, "How do you mean?"

Farrow spoke without hesitation. "I mean do you want the rough stuff or do we talk?"

Yessov shrugged. "For me we talk, Mr. Farrow, and may I congratulate you on your Russian?" He hesitated and then said, "If I remember rightly you married a very pretty Georgian girl. But your accent is all Moscow."

Farrow pressed the pencil into the soft arm of the

chair. "No, I didn't marry her, Yessov. Your people in East Berlin killed her a month before my leave was due. My mother came from Leningrad, but the two KGB men who keep our Russian up to date both came straight from Moscow." He tapped the pencil on his front teeth. "Why are you here, Yessov?"

"Ah, now. Have you heard of Operation Snowball?"

Farrow nodded.

Yessov looked taken aback. "When did you first hear of it, Mr. Farrow?"

Farrow's eyes half closed. "Comrade, you keep talking. It's your turn."

"Can I ask you one question before I talk?"

Farrow sat up and nodded. "Sure."

"Who tipped you off about me?"

"Your boys tipped me off."

"Who exactly, KGB or—" Yessov didn't finish. He was riding his front teeth on his bottom lip. "Mr. Farrow, I think it was not our intelligence section. I think it must have been a Colonel Gouzenko."

Farrow chuckled and put down the pencil. "Let's talk now, Yessov." And they did.

He didn't wait for the two hours; he was back on the small radio twenty minutes later. Anders was not available even by link, so Farrow left a message. "Tell Anders Snowball is for real. The intelligence operation is a decoy. It's a military operation and the wagons are ready to roll."

When Anders got back to Studio Jason it was 7 P.M. and there was a new pile of paper. Reports and intercepts. And a copy of the late edition of the *Evening Standard*.

The headline was "Whose Finest Hour?" and there was the lead story continued on page three and in the stop-press column about the Americans and the Canadians and documents that would show that they betrayed their European Allies in their most extreme peril. He switched on the radio and the BBC seven o'clock news was still on the story and it was already sixteen minutes into the news. They'd obviously started. He switched off and started reading the reports.

There were now eighteen Russians with the Frenchmen at the Temple house and there were four cars there and a Land-Rover. There were three more cars at a garage in Marlow and one at a house in Chiswick. Signals had intercepted a radio message to Rudenko via the Polish Embassy instructing him to telescope phases two and three of Operation Snowball. Long before Anders got Farrow's message he had instinctively guessed that the operation was being speeded up and that it was cloaking some other operation. He got Farrow's message at 9:20 P.M., and already there had been special bulletins on the BBC about statements from shop-floor leaders at Chrysler's at Coventry, recommending strike protests against capitalist conspiracy and particularly US operations in the United Kingdom. The Foreign Office had declined to comment on any aspect of the affair, but it had been noted that the Prime Minister had left his box at the Festival Hall half an hour before the concert ended. Anders used the MGC and parked it in the main quadrangle of the House of Commons after showing his pass to the duty sergeant. Sir John was already in the lobby, and when Anders arrived he nodded to the messenger and they went up to the Prime Minister's room.

The Home Secretary was with the PM and he ignored Anders and Sir John, looking at his papers as the PM read out a PA-Reuter dispatch from Berlin. The Russians were complaining that British Intelligence had blatantly kidnaped a Soviet official in broad daylight. The PM didn't look too pleased when he looked over at Sir John. "What's all this, Sir John?"

"Our man in East Berlin was given a tip-off by the Russians. It concerned a man named Yessov, a senior KGB civilian closely concerned with Snowball. I think we can ignore this dispatch, sir. They've probably put it out as a routine cover as a piece of insurance in case something goes wrong."

"Such as what, Sir John?"

"When the details of Operation Snowball came out, Yessov could link them with it and they fingered him for one of our men in Berlin. This could be pressure on us to use him and then dispose of him."

The Home Secretary winced, rather overdoing it, and the PM said to Anders, "This man Rudenko. Whose orders will he carry out if the KGB and the army are in conflict?"

"He'll carry out KGB orders, sir, but if the army people want to override him they'll send someone important enough to control him."

There was a knock on the door and the PM's Parliamentary Secretary came in and put a message slip on the PM's desk. When the PM had read it he passed it to Sir John. It said, "Commissioner of Metropolitan Police to PM. Explosion at US Embassy, Grosvenor Square. South entrance and wall badly damaged. No casualties. Demonstrators now assembled but under control. Ends."

Sir John passed it to Anders, who read it and didn't look surprised.

The PM said, "Sir John, do you feel we should crack down now or see if it dies down?"

Sir John raised his eyebrows to Anders. Anders hesitated, then said, "I think we should finish them off now, but I suggest you leave it as part of my operation and the police only deal with organized breaches of the peace."

The PM stood up. "Sir John, it's yours for another

two days. I agree with Anders. If he can cope it will save a lot of diplomatic bruising. If you can't cope in two days, Anders, I shall pass it over to the army. It's almost more their pigeon already, but if we use them there will be questions in the House and I'd like to avoid that at the moment. I shall inform the Leader of the Opposition tonight."

Anders drove to Grosvenor Square. There were small groups of demonstrators still there and smaller groups of sightseers attracted by the lights and the TV cameras. He saw Commander Bryant talking to a chief inspector and walked over to them. Bryant saw him and said, "Hello, Anders, this lot must be part of your operation."

Anders nodded. "Have you identified any of them?"

Bryant laughed. "Oh, yes, there are three or four of the old gang here. There are two we've been watching for you, and Rudenko drove slowly past about ten minutes ago." He looked quizzically at Anders. "Getting a bit out of hand, isn't it?"

Anders didn't reply as he looked over the crowd. Then he said, "I'd like a meeting at my place at six A.M. if you can make it, Bryant."

Bryant nodded. "I'll be there."

The BBC headlines at midnight said that there had been spontaneous meetings in Birmingham and ten thousand car workers at British Leyland would be striking for two days in sympathy with Chrysler workers. Production of British Leyland's new export-only Jaguar sports car, the XK-157, would be at a standstill. Production at Longbridge worth £19 million would be lost. A US airbase in East Anglia had been attacked by a mob of villagers. Two arrests had been made. The US Ambassador had had his car attacked as he was leaving a dinner of the Anglo-American Chamber of

Commerce at the Dorchester Hotel. Enough damage had been done to necessitate His Excellency's leaving the car under police escort and returning to the hotel. University students had demonstrated against an American professor addressing the students' union. He had had to abandon his talk. Anders switched off the radio and walked into the signals and operations room.

When Rudenko received the instructions to telescope phases two and three he had asked for a confirmatory repeat and he'd got it an hour later. Loussier had given the story and the documents to the *Evening Standard* and had neither asked for nor received payment. Rudenko's instructions were to get the story printed as quickly as possible even in some vague form. All Rudenko wanted was the excuse, the peg on which he could hang the demonstrations and the explosions. He had called in all the rough boys to the house at Temple. The three explosives men were at separate houses in the London area. One thing that worried Rudenko was that he'd been given a new call sign and a different frequency. It was a frequency in the wave band used by the Red Army, not by the KGB. But everything else was routine and normal.

22

ANDERS HAD WORKED all through the night, and at five thirty he walked from the studio into the cobbled, sloping yard. He took several deep breaths. The cold air caught at his lungs and the early morning mist was damp on his unshaven face. He knew he would feel better when he had bathed and shaved but he wanted to delay this pleasure and comfort, for that would mean the die was cast and all the moves and countermoves of the next two days would be inevitably set in motion. Anders knew that after Yessov's revelations there would be vigorous diplomatic moves at the highest level. By now all NATO governments would have been alerted and troops all over Europe would be standing to under the impression that it was part of some surprise military exercise.

There was an iron stairway up to the roof, and Anders slowly made his way up the rusty steps until he stood on the flat roof of the studio building. It had a false wall all around the top to conceal the festoon of aerials and power cables that littered the roof. He half smiled at three geraniums in pots put there by his driver, who despite his loyalty and efficiency thought that Anders' work was living proof of the folly of man. No doubt these potted plants were meant to weave their spell of ordinariness and bring a touch of normality to the madness that went on in the building below. Anders looked southeast to the Thames, and the early morning light colored the buildings on the South Bank. It was going to be warm. The light was at the morning end of the spectrum and a rosiness touched whatever was white on the buildings. The atmosphere was clear and the sky was nearer green than blue. The river and its buildings awaited Canaletto. A tug pulled three flat coal barges, empty of their load, and riding light and uneasily as they met the wash of a River Police launch that was plowing its purposeful way against the falling tide. There would be traffic like this this morning on the Moskva River, the Vistula, the Don, the Seine, the Rhine, and the Danube, and in elegant buildings along their banks men would be planning to unleash those straining dogs of war. Robins staking out their winter territory, wolves breathless in the snow, red tongues hanging loose from white teeth frothed with their saliva, panting as they waited for a leader to decide what to do. There was early morning lorries using the Embankment, hoping to clear the sprawling mass of London before the main roads funneled the commuter cars into the City and the West End. He heard the faint heavy chimes of Big Ben; he had a quarter of an hour to bathe and shave. As his footsteps clanged and echoed on the iron stairs he released the brake on his mind and thought of the girl. If he was lucky she would be free by tomorrow night. He dismissed the undisciplined thinking. It had nothing to do with his luck; it was his skill and thinking that would save her.

When he had finished shaving he used the backs of his fingers to clear the steam from the mirror, and with the cheap comb halfway to his hair he noticed his face. The brown eyes were staring, not looking, his mouth was tight, and there were lines at the corners that were mere creases of determination. The nose had flaring nostrils, as if it needed more air than it could normally get. He knew he wasn't that ugly, but the face was like those of ordinary men that newspaper photographers catch in some halfway house of movement that makes all men look criminal or demented. He stroked the comb a couple of times through his hair and slowly lowered his hands. For once he felt resentment at the system. He didn't deserve a face like that, hollow cheeked and with a madman's eyes. He looked down for some reason at his shoes and saw the concrete floor. And as he looked down he was alone and afraid and he couldn't remember what had happened since he'd waved good-bye to his mother after the wedding. He hadn't known as he waved what he was going to do; he just did it. And now it was like a finger pressing on a delicate train of clockwork gears, forcing it to breaking point. He could hear people arriving for the meeting and he shook his head and tied his tie.

He walked into the room smiling and waved the half-dozen people to the plain wooden chairs around the army-issue trestle table. He looked around the table and said, "I think everybody knows everybody else with the possible exception of Jake Salis. Jake is our liaison to CIA, both here in London and direct to the States."

Jake Salis gave a general nod or two to the rest of the table and Anders half turned in his chair to point at the wall behind him.

"On the wall, gentlemen, there is a map of the UK, and it is pinned and flagged with known Communist operators. The pink pins are casuals and the red ones full-timers. Blue are actual KGB and yellow are actual GRU. For those who are not familiar with the functions of the GRU, there are Xerox copies of a report available for you. The next map is a large-scale map of an area on the Thames called Temple. It's really an outlying piece of Marlow, but as it is on the south bank it falls under Maidenhead for administration and local authority and police liaison. Marlow comes under High Wycombe. Next to the map are photographs of Mill House at Temple and floor plans, brought up to date, including apparent disposition of personnel and arms and ammunition. This is being used by the other side as an operational base. The small photographs are people known to be based there, and they include the two Frenchmen. The large photograph is of Rudenko, the KGB man who is in charge of their side of Operation Snowball. The girl is SIS on loan from Paris. She penetrated the French group, but as you know she was picked up by Rudenko.

"When this started we saw it as a combined operation between a group of anti-English, anti-American Frenchmen and a combination of the Polish security police Z-Eleven and the KGB. The object appeared to be to cause ill will in the NATO alliance against the United States and Canada. The final objective was the withdrawal of US troops from NATO. We now know that Snowball has an even more serious purpose. We have obtained from a defector the actual operational instructions for a unit of the Red Army which covers its warlike advance to Hannover. Similar instructions have been issued to many other units—maybe all units; we just don't know at this stage. The KGB and their man here, Rudenko, are not aware of the nature of phase four of Snowball, and we are as yet uncertain of their reaction if and when they are told. Our instructions are to contain the operation here, and that means a coordinated roundup of forty-three men and seven women. There is also the opportunity of dealing in some way with collaborators—but that is entirely for Special Branch to decide, and I believe they are meeting MI-5 on the subject later this morning.

"Now let me introduce you to Colonel Fellows, who is providing a special infantry unit for this operation. These men are heavily armed with good weapons and the Mill House is already something of a fortress. Colonel Fellows—Jake Salis of CIA; James Kent and Roger de Freitas, both from the Foreign Office; Commander Bryant, Special Branch; Blair Logan from the PM's office; Wing Commander Pallin from the Ministry of Defense; Lieutenant Sanders, Security Signals; and Bill Macdonald, SIS Paris and Metropolitan France.

"Although it's open for brief discussion I have planned on these lines. Commander Bryant will deal with the listed collaborators and activists who are either resident here or diplomats accredited here. I will act as coordinator and concentrate on the Russians with the help of Colonel Fellows. James Kent and Roger de Freitas will cover all liaison with foreign governments and keep us in touch with the FO's requirements. I'd like to ask the Wing Commander to keep himself free to check with the FO and MI-Six on the state of the game in Moscow. Mr. Sanders will be carrying out his normal duties, and Mac will be with me.

"There are several copies of dossiers on all known people involved laid out on the trestle table along the far wall. Unless there are particular questions at this stage, I'd like you to get up to date on the material and" —he looked at his Rolex—"I suggest we meet again at ten A.M. sharp in this room. My people have marked the rooms which are available for each section, and all the usual facilities are laid on. Right. Any questions?"

Jake Salis half raised his hand and said, "I checked about midnight with the NSA and they report only slightly higher levels of signals traffic in the Soviet Union so far as the Armed Forces are concerned. However, where there is increased traffic it's significant that not only is it in units in Poland, Hungary, Czechoslovakia, and the western borders of the Soviet Union but also that the units involved have above-average vehicle strengths and are therefore maximum mobile."

172

Somehow this statement brought the position home more vividly than all the situation reports had done. There were a few moments of silence as people absorbed the information and its implications.

Jake Salis looked around the table as he leaned back, apparently indifferent to the reactions. After a few moments he said, "The President has had the Think Tank going full speed on this situation since we first got the information through your SIS man in East Berlin. Their current assessment is that the Red Army has not been committed irrevocably to phase four of Operation Snowball. If there is no leak from Yessov back in Moscow and no leak from your outfit in East Berlin and no leak from us here, and, I guess, if we can clobber Rudenko and his boys before they set up a situation that's so attractive to the Red Army that they are tempted to cash in, they may not operate phase four. Seems to us vital to find out what would have marked the end of phase three so finally or so decisively that the generals felt it was worth waiting for. Our view is that they wanted reasonably general chaos, starting and concentrating in the UK, and maybe a high level of anti-Yank feeling." He shrugged. "We'd be interested in any alternative thinking."

Anders nodded. "Thanks, Jake. The PM's office is responsible for our situation evaluation. You can deal direct with them. If they mess you about let me know."

Anders had realized as Jake Salis was speaking that there was a big hole in the US thinking. Gouzenko had actually fingered Yessov and the KGB would work that out and be looking for the old tiger the moment he got back to Moscow, and although they wouldn't know what it was all about and why he'd fingered Yessov, it wouldn't take long to break him open and then the fat would be in the fire.

The scraping of chairs being pushed back cut

through Anders' thoughts, and as he walked with Bill Macdonald up the narrow corridor to his office he rapped on one of the doors and said over his shoulder, "That's yours, Mac," and Macdonald took his two light cases into the room as Anders marched on. Anders read quickly again through Farrow's report and then walked down to the signals room. The red lights were on and the two sergeants were wearing their headphones and taking down messages on the signal pads in front of them. Anders moved to the small soundproof booth and beckoned Lieutenant Sanders into the small cabin. "Sandy, I want to speak to Ed Farrow in Berlin. How soon can you fix it?"

"Morse or voice?"

"Phone."

"You'd have to use the single side-band matching sine-wave job. I can rig it for you in about four minutes but it's not entirely secure."

"Who can eavesdrop?"

"Well, everyone and no one. I don't think they've cottoned on to it yet, but if they rumble the basics then it's easy to break the rest."

"Let's have it then, Sandy."

Two minutes later the sine waves were coinciding on the number-thirty gelatin, and after the identity checks Anders took over.

"Ed, you mentioned a Colonel Gouzenko, the guy who tapped your KGB friend. Is he still under surveillance?"

"Yes, Tad. By the way, he's the official liaison between Red Army Command, the KGB, and GRU. Appointed way back, long before Snowball was dreamed up."

"Fine, Ed, fine. I want Gouzenko taken to the cleaners. Is that understood?"

"You mean all the way, Tad?"

174

"Yes, if necessary, and as soon as possible. As tidy round the edges as possible, and if it can't be done completely clean don't let the light fall on the KGB. Rather on us than them. Is that understood?"

"Yes. You can ask West Berlin to give me a full rundown on Gouzenko. Everything we've got that'll help me."

"Let me know when you've dealt with it, Ed."

"OK, Tad. How are things your end?"

"All under control. Ending transmission now."

Back in his office Anders listened to the headlines at the end of the BBC news. All the other national newspapers had taken the *Evening Standard* story as the main lead; only the *Morning Star* gave it no mention at all.

The *Daily Express* had taken the story over from its evening stablemate—there was no other story on the front page—and the account carried over to page three with more photographs on page four. There was a photograph of Churchill at a BBC microphone under a banner headline, "We'll Fight on the Beaches." Both Mackenzie King and Roosevelt had pictures and biographies, but the rest of the newspapers had all that. What sold an extra million copies of that day's *Daily Express* was right slap in the middle of the front page, the circulation manager's joy and the layout man's despair—a full-size copy of the document spread across four columns. In a large panel were the gathered comments of officials and experts from all over the world. There were three short paragraphs that stood out in bold type. At the personal request of the Prime Minister, Beaverbrook Press had made the letter and other documents available to the Cabinet office. A paper expert from Bowaters had expressed some doubts about the authenticity of the paper on which the letter was typed. An official from the United States Embassy had confirmed that the President's signature appeared to be genuine, but all voices agreed that it was only in the forensic laboratories that the matter would be definitely settled. The *Daily Express* warned its readers against a government whitewashing campaign. The readers' interests were to be protected by Chapman Pincher himself, examining the scientists' reports. On page four there was a rather shaky picture by satellite of newsmen crowding around the White House press secretary as he read a short prepared statement to the effect that the President cautioned the public and the media against once more jumping to conclusions without waiting for the facts. In the final edition of the *Express* there had been reports of a demand for a Senate committee to investigate "these wild and baseless allegations" and a report of overloading of Senate telephone facilities by calls from all over the country demanding an immediate Presidential denial of the story. The British Ambassador to the United States was tracked down to the Sparkman and Stephens yard, where he was supervising the varnishing of his twenty-year-old sloop. He was quoted carefully and verbatim as saying, "A damn silly story if you ask me, old boy. If you'd believe that you'd believe anything. You press chappies are always coming up with some bloody story or other." And he'd last been seen sticking a knife into the deck near one of the hatches. The story was generating its own steam and it was going to last for weeks if it didn't get settled decisively in the next forty-eight hours.

A million workers were due to vote on protest strikes during the day. A sharp protest had been made by the Musicians' Union at the inclusion of an American soprano in the role of Madame Butterfly in the new season at the Old Vic. A variety of MPs had given their interpretation of the situation, and several of each party had been publicly rebuked by their party whips.

There had been a bomb scare at Spaghetti Junction in Birmingham, and the Soviet Ambassador had been ordered to the Foreign Office in the early hours of the morning. All TV schedules for the evening had been revised to include special editions of *Europa* and *World in Action,* according to channel. The US Ambassador had declined to comment on the story and the Pentagon, when called, had said they had not yet had the opportunity to read the story and therefore declined further comment. Editors reported an unusual flow of letters to the editor, and some of the longer toothed had written short editorials indicating that there were disturbing indications that the letters came from five or six areas in abnormal quantities. Visiting TV personalities from both the United States and Europe had unfortunately not had time to read the story but they reconfirmed their love of England, the white cliffs of Dover, and the Metropolitan Police.

23

PHOTOCOPIES OF THE GOUZENKO file came over to Farrow within the hour. There were only two quarto pages. There were his promotions and some of the posts held during his long career in the Red Army. From the records Gouzenko had been married with two sons. His wife and both boys had been killed by the Germans. One son was killed just outside Leningrad, and his wife and the other son, at home on leave from an amputation, had been slaughtered by the Germans' 258th Infantry Division as it penetrated the Moscow suburb of Khimki. Gouzenko had been an excellent all-round athlete in his time and was now president of the Red Army boxing association. He had been born in Kazakhstan in October 1909. Lived in humble quarters at the main Kremlin barracks when in Moscow. Many friends, all in the Red Army. Drank heavily but never drunk. Possibly homosexual. Seldom traveled outside Soviet Union, and then only on official business.

Farrow read through the report on Gouzenko's movements during the last twenty-four hours. He had spent the morning at the Military Police barracks, which he appeared to have made his headquarters in East Berlin. After lunch an official army limousine had carried Gouzenko and his bags about a quarter of a mile to a typical suburban street with small detached houses set in small gardens. He had been lodged at a freshly painted house which had been taken over by the Red Army for visiting firemen from Moscow and Warsaw Pact countries. It was a pleasant old-fashioned house without great security precautions. There was generally one private walking in the garden, rifle carelessly slung muzzle downward in unorthodox ease. It had been noted that not long after the car had left, Gouzenko came out and spoke to the soldier, who adjusted the sling on his rifle and carried it from then on in the correct shoulder position. There was a small wooden structure near the front gate that housed the guard at night in inclement weather. Obviously the guard was more routine and courtesy than real. Farrow decided he needed more background on Gouzenko before he lifted him from the house. Anders was obviously in a hurry, but the information he was to obtain was vital and useful only if it was accurate. Out of their interrogations would come Gouzenko's and Yessov's analysis of what their masters would do when they discovered their own different intentions and the fact that they had been discovered by their Western enemies. He had found Yessov ready to talk when he guessed that he had been betrayed deliberately and coldheartedly by Gouzenko.

The early afternoon sun scorched through the window and lay over the dishes of fruit till they looked like Dutch still lifes. Dust specks shone in the shafts of light. With the addition of warmth from the tiled stove the room was cozy, and both men had enjoyed their lunch.

Yessov was twisting and turning the thin stem of his wineglass as he spoke. "One of the problems that both sides face is the question of recruitment and training. We can pick our recruits from youngsters who have had long years as children in one party organization or another. We don't have to teach discipline as they do in any army. But our problem comes later. We have to train our people about the world outside the USSR: other beliefs, other ideologies, other freedoms. That's our great area of doubt and error.

"You people are the other way round. You have to pick by instinct. You've no criteria; it's as wasteful as mother nature and natural selection. You choose people from the 'right' background, the 'right' social class, the 'right' education; that's why you are so shocked and surprised at defectors. You find it unbelievable that a chap from a good school and a member of a good club with a job in the government could be a traitor. A queer—yes. A drunk—yes. But a traitor—no. Actually both sides react rather like this, but because you are so emotionally involved you are more spiteful than we are. You don't even want your defectors back; you'd be embarrassed if they did come back. When one of your men asks a Moscow journalist for the cricket score it's a surprise, an affront.

"We want our people back and we know they'll miss Russia. They'll be punished but they won't be an embarrassment." He hesitated, then looked across at Farrow. "Yet in a way your system produces almost the same end product as ours. All over the world we feel more at home with our counterparts than our countrymen. I've got more in common with you or a CIA man or a German Abwehr man than I have with an average citizen of my country." He leaned back and lifted a silver cruet and slowly turned it so that the light flashed on the facets of the cut-glass containers. Looking across the table, he said, "There's no need to mess about, Mr. Farrow. Sooner or later you're going to ask me about comrade Gouzenko."

Farrow leaned back too and smiled. "Do you know much about him, Yessov?"

"Nobody knows much about him." He gave a short laugh. "I think that's mainly because there isn't really much to know."

"Our records indicate that he may be homosexual."

Yessov shook his head. "No, definitely not." He grinned. "In fact, he's a bit of a stud for his age."

"How do you know?"

"Well, most sections of power in the USSR, and particularly the army, accept that senior people are going to have sex needs, and the army, or whoever, would rather their men get it without behaving like fools with some young girl, so there is an agency for this."

"And Gouzenko uses it?"

"Yes. I don't want to exaggerate, but he's what you could call a regular."

"And if he wanted boys?"

Yessov raised his eyebrows. "If he wanted them he could have them."

"What about money, has he got much?"

"He'll have a fair amount tucked away. Well off, not rich. He spends very little." Then, almost shyly, Yessov said, "I gather you are looking for a weak spot for pressure. It isn't money or women, that's for sure—family he hasn't got, so that narrows the field considerably."

Farrow got up from the table and stood looking out the window onto the garden. The sunshine had gone, it was dusk, and there was a thrush singing in the early evening peace. He opened a window and the bird's song was louder, with a background of traffic in the distance, and nearer to hand someone was mowing a lawn. Farrow spoke without turning. "And what about you, Yessov? What do I use to get your cooperation?" He swung around quickly and watched Yessov's face.

Yessov put his head on one side and looked again at his wineglass. "Mr. Farrow"—and then he looked up —"I tried to tell you just now we fellows are all the same. My weaknesses are universal: money, pretty girls, power—that's what we fall for. We take it, the money and the girls, because we already have the power. I am sure that somewhere in East Berlin there is some pretty girl you sleep with—and probably another in West Berlin when you take two days' leave to see your director." He shrugged elegantly. "And I would guess there is one in London. Probably not so pretty, not so sexy, but one you could marry. And as for money—well, you operate across the Berlin wall so there are cigarettes, coffee, and all the rest of it. Who cares except us? Your people probably know and turn a blind eye to keep you happy. Your official funds are more scarce than ours. But you didn't really have doubts, Mr. Farrow, did you? I'll cooperate because what is happening to Snowball is a disaster. The Red Army will end fighting the Party and the KGB, and *that* would be disaster. Nearly as big a disaster as the Red Army moving into NATO areas. So what is it you want?"

"I want to find from Gouzenko what the Red Army will do if it knows that all NATO heads of government now know about phase four and are ready. Do we need to tell the Party and watch them fight it out?"

Yessov crossed his legs and lit a cigarette. "Comrade, that would be the end." He looked up with sharp hard eyes. "Don't kid yourselves that you would stand on the sideline and watch the blood flow; you would get involved. Whoever won would have to finish NATO—unless Peking got involved and that would finish things for all of us. Who then would be the barbarians? No, you have no choice, no more than comrade Gouzenko has; he's got to get the Red Army to back away." He wagged a warning finger. "And it's got to back *away*. If you make it back *down*, then we might as well dig our graves in your garden now."

"How do we do that?"

Yessov shook his head and pursed his lips. "God knows, comrade Farrow, I must leave that to you. You know what's in your hand of cards, I don't."

And that was true and Farrow knew he had too little time. They had to pick up Gouzenko and quickly.

There were—and to be truthful, still are—articles of clothing issued to Her Majesty's soldiers called: drawers, woolen, long. There are respectable businessmen who served in 1939–45 who still think nostalgically of this underwear as soon as winter sets in. There are others who still wear these artifacts, and Colonel Gouzenko was one of them. And he was wearing them when the light flashed in his eyes and he turned uneasily in his sleep. Farrow had to shake him before he came awake, and then the old warrior sat up, squinted into the light, and said testily, "Get out of here, soldier, get back to your duty."

"Get dressed, comrade Gouzenko."

Only then did Gouzenko sense that something was wrong. He put a hand up to shade his eyes. "Who the hell are you? My God, there's going to be trouble when I—" Then he saw the Luger. He swung his feet to the floor and stood up. Farrow was still in darkness, but he used his torch to help Gouzenko find his clothes and dress.

When Gouzenko was fastening his collar catches Farrow said softly, "Colonel, we are going outside, through the garden to a car. We have no need to harm you unless you try to escape or try to raise the alarm. Both moves would be quite useless, but it would mean we should have to render you senseless. Is this understood?"

The old boy wiped a hand across his mouth, a sort of defense action. "No point in a lot of nonsense, but there are going to be serious consequences for you, my lad, whoever you are."

Farrow led Gouzenko to a break in the beech hedge and bundled him into the car. He waved the driver off and walked back to the house. The old boy had made no attempt to pack his bags or claim personal belongings and had probably hoped that his captors would be diverted. Nearly twenty minutes later Farrow gently closed the house door. There was a big moon—the hunter's moon—and a blackbird sang a few notes as if uneasy. The other car was waiting for him.

Gouzenko was sitting with one arm on the table. The top buttons of his tunic were undone. His face was blotchy and he didn't look too good. Farrow waved the guard away and poured out a couple of straight whiskies from a bottle of Glenfiddich. He pushed one over to the colonel, who smelled it first and then drank it down. Farrow waited as the color came back into the old man's cheeks.

"Colonel, you and I have a lot to talk about. Shall we start?"

The rather protruding eyes were bloodshot and wet but the mouth was pugnacious. "Who are you, young man? I'm not even sure from the way you talk that you're a Russian. You've got some sort of accent."

Farrow smiled. "Comrade, there's nothing amuses me more than a good soldier from the autonomous state of Kazakhstan talking about other men not being Russians."

The old boy laughed, with his head on one side and a rather crafty look. Kazakhstan was bigger than all Europe put together. Not so gay as the Georgians, not so mercenary as the Armenians, nevertheless the good people of Kazakhstan spent a lot of time pointing out to the Soviet world that the Russians were pretty small beer when compared with their brothers in Kazakhstan. He nodded his head. "So you know where I was born, comrade."

"Colonel, I'm a British Intelligence officer and I

must tell you that I know about Operation Snowball."

Gouzenko's shrewd little eyes were looking at him and they were very alert. He went on.

"And I know about phase four too."

Gouzenko's head jerked up and he said, "It must have been Yessov—that bastard Yessov—" and then he frowned. "He must have known, then—must have known when he came here to Berlin."

Farrow nodded. "Yes, he knew."

"Then why didn't he tell the Party or the KGB?"

"As soon as he guessed, he came here to see you, but before he had the chance you had informed certain people, who informed me, and he was picked up."

"How much does Yessov know?"

"Of phase four?"

"Yes."

"Enough, colonel, enough."

He put both hands up to his face and slowly rocked backward and forward.

Farrow said quietly, "Comrade colonel, I think we should talk."

The colonel's face looked drained and haggard and his hand on the table was trembling as he reached for the glass. Farrow poured more whisky and said, "Do you want them to fight it out, colonel?"

"Who—fight—what fight?"

"Do you want the KGB and the Party to take on the Red Army in self-protection?"

The old man sighed. "Of course not. The Chinese would be at our throats in twenty-four hours." He looked up at Farrow. "You're going to tell the KGB or send back Yessov to tell them."

"Would they believe Yessov?"

"Oh, yes, my God, they'd believe him. They wouldn't need to believe anyway. When we are so near to H-hour there is no chance of hiding much if the

185

other side is suspicious. Did he really keep it to himself?"

Farrow ignored the question. "Why do you think he came here—to East Berlin?"

Gouzenko shrugged and let his hands fall to his knees. "To tell the West—you people—our enemies."

"In fact he came to talk to you, to try to prevent this holocaust." Gouzenko seemed stunned by the lightning that had struck him, and finally Farrow said, "Colonel, what are the circumstances of phase three that make the start of phase four inevitable."

"What do you intend to do? Why should I tell you? You will only want to make things worse."

"Colonel Gouzenko, when you have had time to reflect on all this you will realize that if my people wanted to make things worse we should not be talking to you. A phone call to your ambassador in London, or direct to Moscow, and we need do no more. So tell me about phase three of Snowball."

"Phase four will not start until there have been some days of unrest in the NATO countries about the American pact with Hitler."

"How many days had you planned for?"

"Five or six, at least—maybe ten."

"Who was to decide when the situation was ripe?"

"Rudenko would be reporting to the ambassador in London when he thought phase three was advanced enough and after that it would be up to the marshal."

Farrow spoke too soon. "Which marshal?"

Gouzenko hesitated and then said, "You obviously don't know about him."

Farrow's voice hardened. "What the hell does that matter, you fool? Now tell me—what marshal?"

"Rokossovsky."

Farrow stood at the window and looked out. The false dawn had started and the moon was down almost to the level of distant houses. There was a wind blowing and already there were lights in bedroom windows. The good burghers of the Democratic Republic were getting ready for another day's work. Then it clicked in Farrow's mind and he swung around to Gouzenko.

"Comrade colonel, I want you to inform the marshal that phase four has been uncovered. Uncovered by accident by a senior official of the KGB. Tell him that half a dozen men in the West know—no more. They see no advantages for anybody in allowing the situation to develop. We want an assurance by noon today—Greenwich Mean Time, that is—that all units of the Red Army except those on the Eastern frontier will be stood down. We shall want the marshal to telephone to a number I will give you that this has been done, giving his personal assurance. Do you agree to this?"

"Of course."

"You will inform the marshal that all strategic units will be monitored by us. That we undertake that no information will be passed back to the Moscow authorities."

Gouzenko nodded and shivered.

When Farrow had spoken to Anders they both realized that telephone and radio communications from the house in East Berlin were too limited for so important an operation, and after some discussion with security services it was decided to use the top-secret ASTRA radio. There had only been one slip in the tough security veil over ASTRA. But that slip meant that you could read its basic secret for the expenditure of a few shillings at any one of Her Majesty's Stationery offices. If you ask for a copy of the Marine Broadcasting Offenses Act of 1967 and you read it very carefully you will see that it prohibits all radio broadcasting not authorized by the Postmaster General. When it comes to define broadcasting it states that it means broadcasting by means of sound waves, which seems to be comprehensive enough, but it goes on to state "or by any other means." One would assume that that was gilding the lily—after all, all broadcasting is on sound waves. But ASTRA is a radio that doesn't use sound waves and is not susceptible to radio monitoring. ASTRA broadcasts its sounds on light waves. The ASTRA facility was to link the house in East Berlin with Signals Security in West Berlin and the link to Moscow would be maintained through them. Nobody anywhere could monitor that link, not even the British.

When Gouzenko spoke to Marshal Rokossovsky it was clear that Rokossovsky had already been disturbed by the reported possible leak to an unknown KGB man. After the ultimatum Rokossovsky asked Gouzenko for his opinion and his reasoning. He gave this succinctly. Then there was almost a minute's silence, causing signals officers all over the circuit to check for breakdown. At the end the marshal's voice was firm and decisive. He said that he agreed immediately to the conditions with certain provisos that he would discuss only with the designated person at the special number.

He was transferred at once to Anders in Pimlico. Anders spoke first in Polish, instead of Russian. The marshal sounded faintly amused. Then he stated his conditions. First was that it was accepted that he had no means of cutting off phase three of Snowball, as it was a Praesidium and KGB operation, nothing to do with the Ministry of Defense. That was agreed. Second was that Gouzenko should be released as a reciprocal gesture which would go some way toward pleasing the generals. That was agreed. Third condition was that Yessov was now an acute embarrassment to both sides and would be indefinitely, so Rokossovsky required that he would be eliminated in circumstances that would not embarrass either the Party or the Red Army. No mention of not embarrassing the KGB. That was agreed to.

Anders was asked finally if any phase or aspect of Snowball had been passed to Peking. Anders confirmed that no information had been passed but they had intercepts which indicated that the Chinese Army had reported the imminent transfer of twenty-five Soviet divisions to the Warsaw Pact territories. Then with some minor pleasantries the voices ceased. For a few moments there was the hiss of the carrier wave and then—silence.

Sir John Walker stood up at the end of the radio conversation and said quietly to Anders, "Well that's that. I'll inform the PM at once. So far as Rudenko is concerned I want you to squeeze every last ounce out of this situation. Make the net as wide as you want, and as far as the Russians and the Poles are concerned, as tough as you like. They've asked for it, so let 'em have it!"

For the KGB in Moscow the exercise was gathering momentum as planned.

24

On the BBC's *World at One* it was reported that there had been a two-hour Cabinet meeting during the morning. There had been thirty-five arrests by midday, mainly at demonstrations in London, Birmingham, Coventry, and Liverpool. Three policemen had been taken to the hospital. There had been bomb scares at Pan Am's offices in Piccadilly, and a *Daily Mail* team investigating the source of recent letters to the editor had uncovered evidence that false names and addresses had been given in many cases. A well-known union leader, when asked if it was possible that there was a Communist plot behind the disturbances, had laughed at the idea as a typical "Reds under the bed" scare.

A lot of people in various parts of the country started earning the money they had been getting for years by carrying out the instructions they had received. Many others who had received very little were busy making their small piece of the jigsaw fit.

There had been a bitter complaint by the Soviet Ambassador to the Foreign Office concerning a police raid on the Soviet Trade Mission's establishment in Highgate. The FO had passed on the Home Secretary's apologies and had issued a statement to that effect— with the barbed comment that the ambassador would be informed on any future occasion if it was necessary to investigate commercial premises rented by the Soviet Union.

Anders read hastily through the signal intercepts and noted that Rudenko, who had only just got out of the Highgate premises before the police raid, was now using the Mill House at Temple as his headquarters. There was radio traffic from Mill House to Moscow, Birmingham, Paris, and Cardiff. There was a strong indication that the explosives boys were to be sent out for a wide-ranging fling in two days' time. Sympathetic protest action was requested in Brussels and Stockholm. A signal from Moscow required Rudenko to create maximum effect on "all fronts, physical and psychological," with possible restriction to only two more days for phase three.

In Moscow Rokossovsky passed the word to over two hundred men with the rank of colonel or above. The KGB had checked Yessov's desk and found the two envelopes and their simple contents. They were taken as evidence of mental strain. And when a check was made at the dacha there was evidence of sexual activities after the laboratory tests. Then the car was found at the airport and a full-scale search was instituted. The trail ran out at the airport in Berlin. The KGB didn't like that. There was relief amounting almost to rejoicing when Yessov's body was found near a brothel in one of the better suburbs of East Berlin. But that was not until midnight, and meantime it had caused a lot of friction with the regime in the Democratic Republic.

Gouzenko had been released by Farrow at the airport and had been under surveillance until he caught the plane for Moscow.

There was a demonstration during the afternoon at Southampton. It was against the New Zealand rugby team for not including aborigines among the touring players.

25

ANDERS HAD GIVEN his last orders at ten the previous evening. He'd asked for a call at 3 A.M. With a habit left over from when he first joined the army he shaved before going to bed, and as he shaved he put on a cassette of French songs that he'd enjoyed listening to with the girl. The last one was playing as he pulled off his socks and in his mind he smiled at the memory, even though his face couldn't smile, and the soft voice on the tape was singing a little song called "J'ai ta main." But he didn't let it finish. He switched off the player and lay back in bed. Then, still on one elbow, he looked around the room as if it might never be the same again; then his head was on the pillow. Anders never prayed and never had, he considered praying a coward's insurance, but as he closed his eyes he said, "Please let her be all right." A few moments later he was asleep.

The convoy of six vehicles moved to the Embankment and followed it through to where the King's Road moves down to Fulham. At Hammersmith Broadway it turned west and was joined at the Chiswick overpass by a police motorcyclist. For a time it was alongside Anders' MGC and he could hear the radio traffic on the constable's receiver.

The lights of London Airport looked pale in the first streaks of light from a break in the clouds in the east. Farther on you could just see the outline of Windsor Castle to the south of the M4, then up over the overpass and down the main spur to Henley. Then at the second traffic circle the turnoff to the right and the new bypass to High Wycombe. At the Marlow circle the roadblock was already set up and manned by troops, who looked with curiosity at the occupants of the cars. Then there was the signpost pointing down the lane to Temple.

Farther up the road the suspension bridge at Marlow had been blocked off, together with the road to Cookham. The lane up the hill facing the Mill House was blocked where it met the bypass. The roadblock there was hidden by the low-hanging branches of chestnut trees and clumps of blackberry bushes. Although they were not in sight, there were twenty soldiers occupying the buildings of Temple Farm. The farm's Friesian herd had been moved to an adjoining farm early the previous evening.

Across the other bank of the river there were troops lining the hedges four hundred yards back from the banks.

The Thames Conservancy had closed the lock downstream from Temple at Marlow, below the Compleat Angler Hotel. The hotel itself had been evacuated and was now operations and communications headquarters for Anders. Upstream the lock at Marsh had been closed and both banks were covered by troops. At the lockkeeper's cottage at Temple the family had been evacuated, but the lockkeeper was there to advise about river conditions if this became necessary.

Just north of Marlow town was Booker, an old RAF airfield, now only used by light planes and for veteran car rallies. There were two helicopters now at Booker and a mobile signals unit in a trailer operating a net to the RAF at Medmenham, two miles down the road to Henley.

It was almost seven thirty when Anders finished his briefing conference with the infantry officers and Bill Macdonald came in with the latest reports from the surveillance unit at the lockkeeper's cottage. Anders noticed that the girl had not been sighted for three days and that by 7 P.M. the previous evening there were twenty-five men at the Mill House, excluding the two Frenchmen. Rudenko had been seen, apparently checking the boundaries of the property. He had several times put the binoculars on the lockkeeper's cottage and the catwalk across the weir.

There was normally traffic down the lane past the Mill House to the lines of boats at the moorings, and arrangements were made for one of the boatyard's maintenance vans to be used for reconnaissance.

At the boatyard by Marlow bridge, Anders, Macdonald, and two of the infantry officers looked over a 32-foot Fjord Diplomat with twin Volvos of 150 hp each as a possible assault vessel. On the open sea it would do a nice 27 knots but on the river there was a speed limit of 7 knots. There were twin Morse controls, a compass with a grid, an echo sounder accurate to three inches, the usual navigation lights, and four powerful searchlights. There was a radio fitted in the cockpit, and the cockpit area would hold ten men without affecting the steering.

When they were all aboard the bowline was cast off and with the starboard engine ahead and the port engine in reverse the boat's nose came out into the stream and they turned a full circle and then went under Marlow bridge and along the top of the weir and slid into the open end of Marlow lock. When they were through Marlow lock, the man from the boatyard said

194

to Anders at the controls, "Right, sir, take her up to ten knots till we get into Cookham Reach and then lift her up to about twenty knots." As Anders brought the throttle over, the stem lifted and the boat planed and settled up high as she went through 15 knots to 20 knots. Then at a nod from the instructor he put her into neutral and she settled back on the river. Anders looked across the stern and saw why there was a speed limit. A high, smooth wave was roaring along both banks and you could see it grasping and pulling at great clods of earth which hung and then fell in its wake. The small boats moored to the banks stood on end as the water surged and frothed beneath them. It was almost an hour before they slid back under Marlow bridge and then edged in gently to the landing stage in front of the boatyard. Anders jumped off and took the stern line and knotted it easily to the wooden bollard.

Anders walked from the boatyard across the empty main road to the Compleat Angler. In the big car park he saw that there were several armored vehicles. He saw two Bren carriers, and even as he looked a low-profile mobile gun turned with a spray of gravel and stones as it came off the main road.

Anders phoned the Pimlico number and Sanders said that there had been radio traffic from the Mill House to Moscow and the Russian Embassy in London. The traffic had not yet been decoded. There was a report from NSA HQ in the United States that they were monitoring the Mill House with their London listening post. RAF Boulmer in Northumberland had reported four Soviet submarines proceeding in convoy southward, twenty miles outside territorial waters.

There was a control panel across the end of the long table, and when he'd read the reports Anders flicked on the speakers. The army was using phone, not Morse, and there was no attempt to disguise the reports and

195

commands. From a platoon stationed at the edge of the woods facing the Mill House an officer was reporting the first signs of activity at the house, but it seemed odd to hear the words overlaid with the songs of thrushes and blackbirds and a very loud and angry robin, enraged at the invasion of his territory. Then the voice was softer but quicker. "Alfa calling Delta. One of them is getting in a car—a white mini, license number Oscar Tango Yankee seven six nine four—repeat, white mini—" and Anders listened as the mini came out from the big driveway and turned left for the road to Marlow. They didn't stop it until it was almost at Marlow bridge. Anders smiled. These young army people had all the confidence in the world. They'd guessed he was heading for the bridge so why stop him before? As he approached the bridge they waved him into the main parking lot of the Compleat Angler. Anders walked over to the window and saw the man arguing with a young captain while a sergeant looked on. It was Loussier. The captain took him by the arm and led him out of Anders' sight to the hotel entrance.

Anders gave instructions for the man to be taken into the small annex, where he took over from the captain.

"Sit down, Loussier."

"I must protest. Why am I being detained? I am a tourist and I demand—" Then he screamed. It hadn't been a violent kick, but it landed just on the inside edge of his kneecap. Anders stood waiting till the man had composed himself.

"Where were you going?"

Loussier looked up, his face contorted in pain and fear. "What is all this? What is happening?"

"It's the end of Operation Snowball, Loussier. You are under arrest and will be charged with a number of serious offenses. Now I want some information from you, and I think you are too old to play games. We don't particularly want to hurt you but we won't hesitate if you don't cooperate."

Loussier didn't say anything, but his mouth was open and his breathing was quick and shallow.

"Where were you going?"

"To the post office."

"For what?"

"Mail."

"Who is in charge at the Mill House?"

"The Russian."

"You mean Rudenko?"

Loussier looked surprised that Anders knew the name and even more frightened. He nodded. "Yes, Rudenko."

"What is happening today?"

"Nobody knows. Rudenko is suspicious. He thinks someone is watching from the cottage across the weir."

"Where is the girl?"

Loussier's hand went to his mouth and he said quietly, "In a cellar at the back of the house facing the river."

"Is she guarded all the time?"

He nodded. "She is now. Rudenko is very suspicious of her. He has said if anything more goes wrong it will be proof that she is planted on us."

"Is she alone?"

"Most of the time, except for the guard."

"Where is the guard?"

"He sits in the room."

"How long between changes?"

"Two hours on, two hours off."

"How do you get to the cellar?"

"There's a door and steps in the passage by the kitchen."

"How many men are there at the house?"

"I've no idea. The rooms are full and there aren't anywhere near enough beds."

"Where does Rudenko sleep?"

"He's got a room in the attic. He sleeps there and works there."

"Are they all Russian?"

"There are several Poles, two Irishmen, an Englishman, and another Frenchman."

"You mean Firette?"

Loussier nodded.

"How soon were you expected back?"

"I'm generally not much more than an hour."

About eleven thirty, four men left the house and got into a gray Volvo. The army waited until they were almost at the bypass before they held up the car. One of the men spoke bad English, and when he was told to get out one of the men in the back seat put a revolver on the edge of the door and said something sharp in Russian that the soldier didn't understand. The corporal who had walked up to the car from the rear brought the muzzle of his rifle and the sharp sling mounting across the man's fingers trapped against the metal door. One man ran toward the bank of the river and was shot by a high-velocity bullet from one of the sniper's rifles. There had been a sharp crack, then the man had stumbled as he ran, fallen, tried to rise, and then fallen with his arms pulling at his chest. The bullet went straight through him and thunked into the wooden post of a small bridge on the far side of the river. The wounded man was dead by the time they got him to the ambulance at the end of the M4 spur. The other men were taken to Anders. He saw them one by one and then sent them to Reading jail in a police car.

It seemed that the men had been sent out to look for the mini. They had been issued with arms and told

198

to resist arrest if they were stopped by the police. Nobody had said anything about what to do if stopped by the army. The one in the back seat with the Luger just couldn't tell the difference between a soldier's uniform and a policeman's, and he had four smashed fingers to prove it.

At twelve thirty, two men walked out of the drive and looked up the lane to the Marlow road. They talked sporadically and stamped their feet as if they were cold or cramped. They looked around across the fields, up the hill to the main road. They looked at the clump of chestnut trees, but their gaze didn't linger. Then they walked slowly down the gravel pathway to the moorings. They looked across at the launches moored to the pontoons and to where the weir pulled the long strands of green weed over the stones and against the support legs of the catwalk. One of the men peed at the side of the path and the other man stretched and flexed his arms like an athlete before a race. Then they strolled back to the entrance to the house, between the parked cars, to the main door.

Fifteen minutes later Rudenko appeared at the upstairs windows. In room after room he put binoculars up to his eyes and ranged them slowly across the fields and then the lanes and hedges. The party in the lock-keeper's cottage saw the reflection of his binoculars but they couldn't see Rudenko, as he stayed well back from the windows that faced the river. Ten minutes after this inspection there was a man at every window. The bottom sash had been raised by six inches or so and there was no attempt to conceal the weapons that thrust aggressively out. Anders noted that almost half the full complement of men were needed to mount this defense. A man had been posted in the back seat of one of the cars in the forecourt, and another was walking slowly around the lawns with a submachine gun slung over his shoulder. From time to time he snatched the gun to the firing position and went through a dumb show of spraying some area of the grounds. Anders sent a man to check separately with two of the prisoners about the state of food supplies. They were both quite sure that there was food enough for at least ten days.

By midafternoon Commander Bryant telephoned to say that Special Branch had arrested all the civilians and diplomats on Anders' list. There had been no complaints yet from either the Polish or Russian embassies. The press and the BBC had not been given any information but had obviously put two and two together about the widespread arrests and were not giving much time to the protest strikes. Without the organizing framework the demonstrations and strikes seemed to have become halfhearted and ill supported. There was no mention on radio or TV of the cordon of roadblocks in part of the Thames valley.

The military commander came for a conference with Anders and Macdonald and recommended no action till the following day. He urged, "They're on the alert now, and it means half of them are going to be tired in the morning. They could hang on for an hour or so if we start closing in now and then we should be messing about in the dark. I don't really want that unless you feel it's essential."

"How long do you reckon it will take to finish them off?"

"Well, we've got this problem of the large amount of explosive that has been reported. If it wasn't for that we could lay the place open in ten minutes and then go in and mop up. But we can't use more than small arms under the circumstances, and that could take us three or four hours to keep our own casualties low. I understand there's a girl in there who is under duress—is she likely to be used as a hostage?"

"Yes, they could use her."

"And what do you want us to do about that?"

Macdonald watched Anders thinking and waited for him to speak. "Macdonald and I will go in for the girl before you start your attack."

"Fair enough, Major Anders, if that's what you want. Now, we shall go in at first light, about seven o'clock. How long do you want to be in the house?"

"I'm not sure. Let's say we'll send up a red-over-green Very light when we are clear of the house. If you've had no signal by seven-oh-five you go in anyway."

"Well, we'll synchronize watches here at two A.M. if that suits you."

Bearing in mind where the girl was captive, Anders knew from the maps and the layout of the house that the only direction of approach for him and Macdonald was from the river. It would be easiest to take one of the rowboats moored at the lockkeeper's island. This was the shortest distance, but it would be under continuous observation from the upper windows of the Mill House. It was decided to take a typical green, flat Thames punt and launch it, out of sight of the house, around the sharp bend in the river.

Before the light went Anders drove through the deserted town of Marlow and carefully checked the riverbank that they would have to negotiate in the dark. There were plenty of overhanging branches to give them cover, but they could also be obstacles if they were too low.

Anders stopped in Marlow on his way back to the Compleat Angler. There were police and army patrols in the town to prevent looting, and it had needed the PM's personal intervention with the local authorities to arrange the evacuation. Anders spoke to a chief inspector, who nodded a greeting and said, "I don't know if you've heard, sir, but one of the papers has broken the D notice and we've had to close off all the roads, including the M4—thousands of trippers. They're booking most of 'em for walking on a motorway. Everything going all right, sir?"

"Yes, chief. Have you had any attempted looting?"

"Oh, Lord no, sir, there won't be any trouble like that."

"Where've you put everybody?"

"Oh, some's in the schools in Henley, some's at Reading and Maidenhead. The kids have got three days off school. It's a bit like a cross between the war and a holiday in a way."

Anders walked back down the High Street. The shops were closed and deserted and as he passed the post office it reminded him of the girl when she had just come down here with the Frenchman. The pavements were wide with plane trees and flowering cherries and the leaves were falling now, but the street looked somehow French. The houses had been well preserved and there were cobbles and brightly painted doors. The bridge at Marlow is a small version of the bridge at Hammersmith; its architect was the same. Anders stopped halfway across the bridge and looked upstream. The Fjord was wallowing gently on the boatyard moorings, and facing the chandlery were some two dozen boats for sale: big oceangoing jobs that were used as gin palaces and small 27-footers that pushed their way upriver to Oxford and Osney and downstream to the Thames Estuary. On a normal October evening at dusk there would be families and couples strolling on the banks and the boathouse wouldn't be closed. The fours and eights and single scullers and pairs would be on the river enjoying their solitary sport. Anders could see upstream to the bend in the river, but there was a thin mist rolling down the banks to the water. A yellow-painted helicopter with the roundels of RAF Training Command was signaling by Aldis to the airfield at Booker, and then it swung lazily and headed toward Henley and Wargrave. There were lights on in the boatyard building and on the other side at the hotel. Anders straightened up and walked on. As he got to the end of the bridge he heard the sharp crack of a rifle from upstream at the house. There was an echo and then silence.

By the time he got to his headquarters room at the Compleat Angler a report had come in from the lock-keeper's cottage. One of the Russians had taken a shot at the cottage window and the video camera had been hit. It was thought that it was a touch of defiance by one of the Russians, who had seen the last rays of the setting sun touch the big front element of the mirror lens as it swung into a new observation position on Mill House. They had not exchanged fire and had made no attempt to repair the window.

While Anders was eating with Macdonald, a lieutenant came in and saluted and brought the first news that it wasn't all to be left to them to plan. Two Russians had been caught in different places. They had obviously been sent out to check where the nearest patrols were placed. One had had the misfortune to encounter a marine commando in the hedge down the lane to Marlow. He'd had his throat cut cleanly and efficiently. He was on a disciplined patrol because his face had been blackened and he carried no papers of any kind. The other had fallen more among friends and had a broken arm, courtesy of a Gordon Highlander. "He wouldna' gi'e us his wee gun, sir." He was awaiting Anders' pleasure in the back of a truck.

"Where did you get him, lieutenant?"

"Well, first of all he walked down where the boats are moored, but C Company left him alone and he walked back and started up the hill to the bypass. He came into contact with Corporal Maclean at the edge

203

of the second plowed field. He was under observation all the time, sir."

"Fine, mister, wheel him in."

The man was one of the KGB men who had come ashore at Cardiff. Anders recognized the white smooth burn scar across the left side of his face and neck. The broken right arm hung awkwardly and there was blood on the man's khaki shirt, from his mouth. He was obviously in pain, and beads of sweat stood out on his forehead. Anders motioned the Russian to a wooden chair, but the escort corporal kept his gun pointing at him.

Anders spoke in Russian. "What had you been ordered to do?"

"Find the soldiers and report back."

"To Rudenko?"

The man looked astonished. "Yes. You know about him?"

"What is happening in the house?"

"All men are armed and every room is defended. There is much ammunition and automatic rifles. They will do much damage. They wait for you all."

"Where is Rudenko?"

The Russian shook his head. "Rudenko does not stay in one place; he is very active all over the house. He has many good fighters there."

"When do you expect to be attacked?"

"He thought tonight at sundown. Now he thinks tomorrow morning as soon as light comes."

Anders looked up at the corporal. "Thank you, corporal. Give my compliments to the lieutenant, and this man should go to the hospital at Wormwood Scrubs."

As the man stood up, something about him rang a bell in Anders' mind. He looked as though he had expected more interrogation. Maybe they didn't realize how much was known, but instinct made him tell the man to stop.

204

"What were you told to say if you were caught?"

The man leaned heavily against a sideboard near the double doors.

"Rudenko found out things from the girl this afternoon and he said, 'Tell them she'll die with us. She'll die at first attack.' That is all."

"What things did he find out?"

The man shrugged. "I do not know the details. I just know that he found out that she is a spy for the British."

Anders looked at the man for a long time without speaking. He couldn't bring himself to ask the question but he had to know the answer, and eventually he spoke, looking at the man's face. "How did Rudenko find out?"

The man still had blood coming from his mouth and he swallowed before he could talk. He spoke slowly and softly, almost a whisper. "He let the men use her many times. And then she talked."

26

THE LONG PUNT had been taken up to the wall of the churchyard at Bisham. Watches had been synchronized and Macdonald and Anders had rested for a couple of hours.

The river was smooth as glass and the air was still. A few birds moved and chirped uneasily at the disturbance, and from time to time a fish rose with a plop. The low noise of the weir seemed a long way away.

Macdonald had a small but high-powered police walkie-talkie and the Very pistol and six cartridges. A Luger and clips of cartridges lay on one of the transverse seats. A small Johnson outboard motor lay in the well of the punt, to be assembled by Mac while Anders was on land and then used for a speedy getaway into the shelter of the lock itself.

Anders too had a pistol, and a commando knife strapped to the side of his right leg. Mac had been sitting in the punt for some time, and then Anders said quietly, "Right, Mac, let's go."

They both extended their paddles to push away from the bank. When they were well clear they made slow, quiet, deep thrusts with the paddles and they held them out of the water as the punt glided forward. Once they scraped a shoal of gravel near the bank and once they were forced by growth from an old tree trunk below the surface of the water. It was only a quarter of a mile but it took an hour before they were a few lengths from the first spot where Mill House garden ran down to the start of a small cut at the side of the mainstream. One more quiet dip of a paddle and they slid alongside the bank under the shelter of the flowing branches of a willow, whose dry leaves rustled as they grasped a branch to bring them to a halt. The roar of the weir was loud and continuous. Mac put his mouth to Anders' ear and whispered, "Best of luck, Tad, but wait till your ears have got used to this din."

Anders nodded and Mac held the boat to the bank as Anders stood up carefully and stretched his leg to the bank. Then he stood under the willow tree. He could see the lights in the house. Every room was lit and he could hear shouting as if there was a party. He edged carefully toward the house, putting his feet gently on the smooth lawn. There was the noise of a radio, and he could just tell that it was a news bulletin in Russian from Moscow. He stood listening and that's when it happened. The gun was rammed into his back right against his spine and a voice said in Russian, "Don't move, friend. Just put your hands up and walk slowly to the door—the open door there, at the back of the house."

Anders took two long strides and the gun stayed pressed against his kidneys and he knew he was safe. The man wasn't trained. You get a whole week on getting away from a gun in your back, and for the last two days they use live ammunition. At the end of two days it's easy. But you must have the muzzle right against you. A foot away and it's more difficult; three feet away and it's an entirely different technique. But the gun was tight in his back, digging in hard.

Anders turned, trapped the man's gun arm, and put his other hand across the front of his windpipe in one quick movement. Then he slid his left hand up over the man's mouth and pressed up hard against the center cartilage of his nose. There was a strangled noise from under Anders' hand, and then Anders whispered, "Where's the girl, comrade?" The man struggled in a frenzy and Anders levered the gun arm back up till it would have to break at the shoulder or elbow to go higher. The man's body was bent back, bowed and taut with pain. He groaned each time he breathed, and Anders went cold because he suddenly realized why the man was so frightened. He pulled the arm and it cracked like a chicken bone but loudly and sickeningly.

In a rush of choking words, the man said, "She's dead, comrade. They killed her an hour ago."

Anders pressed the arm still more but it was pointless; the joint had come out at the shoulder and only ligaments held it. "Where is she, you son of a bitch? Where is she?"

The man shuddered. "They put her in the weir an hour ago." His head fell forward and as his body sagged Anders stood back and let him fall. The man lay on his back, his right arm at an impossible angle. The moon shone down palely and caught the man's white face with its staring eyes and wide-open mouth, and it glinted on the dew on the fallen leaves. Anders knelt down and put his big left hand over the man's mouth as his knife went into the left-hand rib cage. The man shuddered and quivered like a slaughtered chicken, and then he was still. Anders fought hard not to put the knife in again and again. Then he stood up and laid his face against the cool smooth bark of the tree. He felt as if he never wanted to have to open his eyes again. He wanted a deal with God, or fate, or whoever decided; he'd had enough and he'd give up the chance of anything good that might happen before he died in exchange for peace and nothingness. Then he heard Mac calling, and he was near.

"Tad—are you there?" Then Mac saw him. "Christ Almighty, Tad, what's the matter? What's happened?"

208

Tad straightened up and held up his face to the moon. "They've killed her, Mac. They've killed her and put her in the weir."

"Are you sure?"

"Yes, absolutely sure." His arms hung loose and he still held the knife. "Let's go, Mac. We'll save the Very lights. No need for them. We'll just punt across to the lock."

And fifteen minutes later hands were stretched down to help them up the iron rungs at the side of the deep lock.

The team at the lockkeeper's cottage phoned through to the operations room at the Compleat Angler. Five minutes later Very lights went up from Marlow and Mac watched Anders' face bathed in the eerie red and green light. The flares seemed to hang glittering in the air for a long long time and then in the thin, misty, early morning light the first shots hit the Mill House and Anders watched as alternate tracers looped their way into the upper rooms. Men who had run in panic into the garden had been brought down in the pounding cross fire from the Bren guns on the far bank of the river. But the men at the windows were firing back accurately and with no sign of surrender. All the windows in the lock-keeper's cottage had gone and tiles were flying from the roof. A steel-clad bullet clanged on a main water pipe and there was a fountain of water pouring down the side of the house. A spray from a machine gun ripped the guttering from the eaves of the roof. Then one of the signal sergeants took off his headphones and handed them to Anders. "It's for you, sir—you personally."

Anders took one phone and pressed it to his ear, the head harness and the other earphone hanging loose. He picked up the hand microphone and pressed the button. "Anders here."

"This is Colonel Gray, Major Anders. I've just had

a radio message from the center of town—Marlow, that is. The chief inspector saw a man he didn't recognize and stopped him. The man laid him out and got away. We think from the description it's this Rudenko fellow. We thought we'd better tell you. We don't want him to get knocked off if you particularly want him alive."

Anders face was unmoving. "How long ago did it happen?"

"Six–seven minutes by now."

"Where?"

"In the High Street. In the doorway of the Vienna Coffee Bar. The man had wet feet. In fact he was wet to his knees."

"Right, colonel. Leave it to me. Warn your people that I shall be there. I want everyone off the streets. If anyone moves I shall take it that it's Rudenko and shoot."

"Do you want supporting fire from us, major?"

"Is there any chance he could break through the cordon?"

"Not a chance. It's getting lighter every minute."

"Well, leave it to me, then. I'll contact you if I need help."

"Roger and out."

Anders had realized halfway through what had happened. Rudenko wouldn't risk getting caught himself and he must have gone down the river, hugging the far side with the mist to give additional cover. He would have used the dinghy that had been moored in the cut. Anders had seen it on his first reconnaissance and he hadn't noticed it was missing when they'd moored the punt. He looked across at the house. A corner of the roof was burning and there was a fire engine parked waiting halfway up the lane on the hill. He could see troops in battle dress herding a group of men into a three-ton truck.

210

Anders turned to Mac. "There's a path from the other side of the lock. Let's take a car and you can take me to the first cordon in West Street."

At the first cordon the Grenadier captain recognized Anders and saluted. Anders thought it must be the first time he'd been saluted in the last seven years. The barrier was pulled aside and the captain said, "The Coldstreams are at Quoiting Square, sir. I'll radio that you're coming."

Anders and Mac got out at Quoiting Square. There was a garage at the corner of the junction and a half-track was facing across both roads.

As they walked over to the command post Anders stopped and turned to Macdonald. "Mac, will you do something for me?"

Mac nodded. "Yes, Tad. You want me to find the girl?"

Anders nodded and then walked alone over to the group at the radio. There was a plump middle-aged captain who was listening on the headset. After a few moments he took off the phones and, smiling broadly, said, "Just had the news that it's all over at the Mill House. They've had seven killed, ten hospital cases, and the rest are as good as new. We didn't sustain a single casualty. Jolly good show, I'd say." The smile faded away as he looked at Anders' face, and he said quickly, "They've spotted the Russian by the cinema, sir. Said I was to tell you."

"Have you got an armorer sergeant, captain?"

"Yes. I'll whistle him up."

The dour-looking sergeant saluted and Anders asked him, "Have you got a Walther pistol, sergeant?"

"Yes, sir, PP or PPK?"

"PP if you've got it."

The sergeant trotted off and was back in a few moments with his offering. He looked up at Anders. "Here we are, sir. You've got the extra round, as you know, eight in the magazine and one up the spout. And how many magazines do you want?"

"Two extra, sergeant."

"Here we are, sir. The pistol was calibrated last week at 100 meters. Did it myself."

Anders took the pistol and stuffed the two extra magazines in his jacket pocket. He turned to the captain. "I don't want any interference from anybody, captain. My compliments to all other town patrol commanders, and let them know my orders."

"Sir!" He flung up an energetic salute, but Anders was on his way.

Marlow's main roads are laid out like a T, and he was walking up the short west part of the top. There was an island and then a right turn down the wide main High Street that he'd walked down once already that night. At the post office he stood still and listened. The town was silent, but a slight breeze ruffled his hair, and it carried the faint sounds of vehicles far away. Then he came to the side road that went to the left, and three hundred yards along was the cinema. He crouched down low and cautiously put his head around to check that the street was clear. Nothing moved, and he crossed the street with a rush to the side of a bakery. He edged along the wall past several shops and then he was at a small cul-de-sac that ran down to the river, where it ended in a gentle slope for launching small dinghies. He ran across to the far wall, and as he backed against it a bullet whipped through the hanging fronds of Virginia creeper and whined off to shatter one of the big glass doors in the cinema. Then he could see Rudenko. He was bent over a small white dinghy. One arm was stretched out with a gun pointing up the street and the other was trying to pull the cord on a small outboard. He tried once and it spluttered to silence and then Anders aimed at the dinghy as it turned against its lines and the whole of the flat square transom was exposed. The first shot was too high and hit the cylinder block of the outboard. The second was still too high, but there was a puff of black smoke and then a small orange flame. The next shot hit the dinghy right at the waterline. It was a glass-reinforced plastic hull and the six-inch hole was untidy and jagged but the dinghy was sinking fast. Rudenko fired two more shots but they were very wide. Then he scrambled up the bank and over a low garden wall. Anders guessed where he would head for and ran back down the side street into the High Street where there was a triangle. It housed a pub and the war memorial and at the base of the triangle was the parish church.

As soon as he was actually in the churchyard Anders went down so that he was protected by the tombstones. And he waited. It was ten long minutes before Rudenko moved and a stone clattered over to Anders' left. He didn't move for a long time and then he looked through a shield of tall grass and wild scabious. Rudenko was only fifteen feet away and he was facing away from Anders, expecting him to have followed down the side street and over the wall. Rudenko's right hand was holding the gun and it was resting on the shoulder of a marble gravestone while Rudenko was maneuvering to observe the long low wall. He was actually turning to look back over his shoulder when Anders fired. The first shot went through Rudenko's right hand and sent the pistol spinning yards away into tall grass, and the second chipped the marble stone. As it whined off across the river Anders saw that a sliver of marble had sliced open a large gash in Rudenko's cheek. Rudenko seemed oblivious to the blood cascading down his face. He just watched Anders coming forward. He must have just seen the flash of Anders' knife before it went in him but that was all. Anders was like a wild animal and he seemed deaf to Mac's shouts as he came stumbling toward Anders across the churchyard. He was still holding Rudenko when Mac got to him. Mac took one look and caught Anders' arm. "Don't, Tad, don't do any more, it's terrible." He looked at Anders' wild, twisted face with the tears streaming down as he fought to get his breath. And he led Anders by the arm, away, back over the bridge to the room in the hotel. "Get out!" he shouted to the gaping soldiers. "Get out, you bloody fools."

When the sergeant and two privates found Rudenko's body it was almost naked and the grass and flowers were dark with his blood. They were silent, and then one of the privates said, "Sarge, Anders must have pulled this bugger's guts out with his hands. Christ, I've never seen anything like this—not ever. He must be bloody round the bend."

At Tilbury docks that night there was drawn up a variety of vehicles alongside the MV *Batory*, which was taking on passengers for a Baltic pleasure cruise and then on to Leningrad. A doctor was handing over medical notes for four stretcher cases. Commander Bryant was handing over the contents of two Black Marias. The coffins had gone aboard earlier so that the passengers wouldn't be disturbed. Nobody was very chatty, but there was no unpleasantness.

Ambassador Borowski was preparing for a party in honor of the Mazowze dancers which the PM was going to attend. And His Excellency was hoping the PM would accept an official gift of a symbolic silver lump of coal from the mayor of Katowice, where the team from England had lost 2–0 the month before.

Macdonald had made a few threats in various directions about what could happen to soldier boys who thought they had seen impossible things. And he'd dusted down Anders, put him in a uniform, and given him a heavy shot of amphetamines. Sir John Walker had been congratulatory all around and suggested Anders take a few weeks' leave.

NSA codebreaker Hank Peters parked his car in the staff lot at Fort Meade and reread the letter from the girl who had said no because she felt he had no real job security.

Bill Macdonald breathed the good dust-filled air of Paris and took the girl who was waiting for him at Orly to Maxim's. "How did the meetings go, Mac?" she asked.
"Not bad," he said. "Not bad."

At 2 A.M. the cassette machine was still on, but it played no music. It had come to the end of the music two hours ago. Anders was asleep and one hand hung down to the floor. He wasn't in his own room, he was next door. There was a note on the floor by his hand, which said, "I've done what you asked about the girl. It's best you don't know any more. Love, Mac."

And on the bedside table was a vase with a dozen red roses. There were a few fallen petals on the tabletop and the roses drooped their heads on the long stems. They were nearly dead but not quite.